G000049294

∽ RETURN ∽

SKYE MALONE

Return
Book Three of the Awakened Fate Series

Copyright © 2014 by Skye Malone

Published by Wildflower Isle | P.O. Box 17804, Urbana, IL 61803

All rights reserved, including the right to reproduce this text and any portions thereof in any manner whatsoever.

This book is a work of fiction. All characters, names, places and incidents appearing in this work are products of the author's imagination or are used fictitiously and are not to be construed as real. Any resemblance to actual events, organizations, or persons, living or dead, is purely coincidental.

ISBN: 1-940617-14-6
ISBN-13: 978-1-940617-14-5

Library of Congress Control Number: 2014906858

Cover design by Karri Klawiter
www.artbykarri.com

PRONUNCIATION GUIDE

Aveluria (av-eh-LUR-ee-uh)

Dehaian (deh-HYE-an)

Driecara (dree-eh-CAR-uh)

Fejeria (feh-JER-ee-uh)

Greliaran (greh-lee-AR-an)

Ina (EE-na)

Inasaria (ee-na-SAR-ee-uh)

Jirral (jur-AHL)

Kirzan (KUR-zahn)

Lycera (ly-SER-uh)

Neiphiandine (ney-fee-AN-deen)

Niall (nee-AHL)

Nialloran (nee-ah-LOR-en)

Nyciena (ny-SEE-en-uh)

Ociras (oh-SHE-rahs)

Prijoran (prih-JOR-an)

Renekialen (ren-eh-kee-AHL-en)

Ryaira (ry-AIR-uh)

Sieranchine (see-EHR-an-cheen)

Siracha (seer-AH-cha)

Sylphaen (sil-FAY-en)

Teariad (tee-AR-ee-ad)

Torvias (TOR-vee-ahs)

Velior (VEH-lee-or)

Yvaria (ih-VAR-ee-uh)

Zekerian (zeh-KEHR-ee-en)

1

CHLOE

Branches snapped beneath my bare feet and only the fact my skin had changed enough to handle it kept the twigs from hurting. A frigid wind rushed through the forest around us and rain drizzled past the trees, the drops feeling so much colder than the water we'd left behind.

"There should be a road soon," I assured Zeke, silently praying it was true. I had no idea where we were, short of being somewhere *way* north of Santa Lucina, but I couldn't believe we'd gone so far as to leave any trace of civilization behind.

Zeke didn't respond. But for the few moments in the water when he'd sent a message to his sister, he'd hardly spoken a word, and when I glanced back, his gaze was locked on the forest floor in a way that made me doubt he was seeing it.

I hesitated and then kept walking. I didn't know what to say. His brother, Niall, was a Sylphaen. He'd murdered Zeke's dad, and nearly killed their oldest brother as well. And barely half an hour ago, he'd kidnapped me to bring me to his master, the 'Wisdom' Kirzan, for some kind of sacrifice. If not for Zeke coming after us and stopping him – and having to kill Niall's accomplice in the process – I'd probably be in the custody of the Sylphaen right now.

On the one hand, I couldn't thank him enough for saving me.

I just didn't know what to do about the rest of it.

Or how to feel about the fact that, the moment we did find civilization, it'd be time to say goodbye.

Letting out a breath, I tried not to give into how much the thought hurt. Living in Kansas, I'd stayed away from the ocean for most of my life. I'd never even come near the sea till I'd snuck out of the house for a short vacation with my best friend a few weeks ago. It'd only been then that I learned I was actually dehaian, a fish-person mermaid thing like in story-books. But that came with problems, one of the biggest of which was the fact that most of my kind could no sooner live on land for an extended period of time than they could fly to the moon. And they couldn't travel far from the ocean either. If they tried, it'd draw them back with a compulsion so strong, it felt like they were going insane.

I knew. It'd happened to me the first time my parents – my adoptive parents, anyway – had tried to bring me back home.

But now that I'd survived changing into dehaian form, now that I'd been underwater and not died from the shock, my half-landwalker heritage meant that I might be able to return to Kansas, and perhaps stay there indefinitely too. Which, considering it'd get me away from Niall and the Sylphaen, was great.

It just meant leaving Zeke.

And the more I thought about it, the less comfortable with that reality I became. I knew there wasn't really a choice, though maybe someday the Sylphaen would be dealt with and I could come back.

But in the meantime... it hurt.

Leaves brushed my side when I skirted past another bush, the feeling strange against the faux-swimsuit covering me – as if the plants were touching my skin, though to all appearances they were running up against an iridescent and vaguely scale-like fabric instead. Shifting my shoulders against the sensation, I continued down the narrow deer trail.

Time crept by as the path twisted through the undergrowth, and only my awareness of the ocean behind us kept me certain we were moving in the right direction. The rain picked up, becoming a steady downpour. My hair plastered to my face and I swiped water from my eyes with every few steps. Mud covered my feet while leaves and pine needles stuck to my legs. The gray sky overhead grew darker as the afternoon turned to evening, and cautiously, I let my eyes take on a hint of the dehaian glow just so I could see through the twilight.

And still the forest remained unchanged.

I swallowed hard as darkness settled around us. I didn't

know what we'd do if we had to spend the night out here. It was true that, as dehaians, we rarely needed to sleep, but I also hadn't managed more than a few nightmare-interrupted cat-naps in almost five days. Even for us, that seemed like it was pushing it, and the exhaustion dragging at my muscles felt like it agreed.

But I really didn't want to sleep on the muddy forest ground. For that matter, I didn't want to sleep at all.

A light flickered in the distance.

My heartbeat picked up speed as my gaze locked on the golden glow flashing behind the windblown leaves ahead. Breathlessly, I turned my head, not taking my eyes from the light.

"Zeke?"

"I see it," he answered, his voice far more reserved than mine had been.

I glanced back to him questioningly.

His mouth a thin line, he hesitated and then twitched his chin in silent agreement for us to go onward.

We continued past the bushes, leaving the deer path finally when it curved away from the light. Branches swiped at me as we picked our way through the undergrowth, and soaked leaves slid like cold, clammy fabric across my skin and scales alike. Wind tossed the treetops as we neared the source of the light, and in the last shadows of the forest's shelter, we paused.

It was a porch light. Affixed beside the green front door of a two-story house, it shone over the yard, revealing a dilapidated shed on the far end and a stack of firewood beneath a blue tarp closer by. In the driveway, an old, cream-colored pickup sat with a camper shell attached to its back. The house itself had once been white, though age had chewed away at the paint on the siding and the shadows swallowed its second story. Light glowed behind the curtains of a single window on the lower level, and as I watched, a shadow passed across it like someone moving within the house.

I glanced to Zeke.

His expression hadn't changed.

"We need a phone," I whispered. "I have to be able to call Baylie or someone to come get me."

He didn't respond for a heartbeat, and then gave a nod. "When they ask, our boat sank. We couldn't save anything."

"Okay."

"And pretend to be cold."

"I am cold."

He looked to me. "Colder."

I hesitated, realizing what he meant. We'd been walking for hours in the rain, the wind and now the dark, all in swimsuits.

If I wasn't dehaian, I'd probably have been freezing.

"Okay."

He nodded again. Drawing a breath, he made the faint glow fade from his eyes, returning them to normal human appearance. He pushed past the last of the branches and headed into the yard.

Swallowing nervously, I let my eyes do the same and followed.

The steps creaked as we climbed to the porch, and beneath the aged gold light of the lamp, I felt painfully exposed in the black night. As Zeke knocked on the chipped surface of the green door, I hugged my arms to my sides, not having to fake my shivering.

A moment passed. Heavy footsteps sounded within the house, coming closer.

The door opened a fraction, affording us a view of a hardwood floor and a burly man, while the smell of dinner cooking spread into the night air. Standing nearly seven feet tall, the man eyed us with alarm that turned to wary suspicion when he ran his gaze over the two of us in our swimsuits.

"Can you help us?" Zeke asked, a hard note of challenge in his voice despite the question.

The man's brow furrowed. He looked past us to the yard, as though checking for anyone else there. "What are you doing out here?"

"Our boat sank," Zeke told him flatly. "We barely got away, but we lost everything. We've been trying to find some-one to help us since we made it to shore."

The man paused. "Your boat?" he repeated as if testing the words for their sound.

"Yeah."

For a moment, the man didn't respond. "Huh. You, uh, you injured?"

Zeke shook his head. "Just cold and tired. We need to call our friends to come get us. Could we use your phone?"

Again, the man hesitated. His gaze returned to the yard, scanning it briefly, and then he nodded.

"I don't have a phone," he allowed. He pulled the door aside. "But, uh, yeah, come on in."

Still hugging my arms close, I followed Zeke in. A sparsely decorated living room waited beyond the door, with a couch covered by brown blankets facing the cold fireplace. A scuffed coffee table sat between them, a dirty plate and an empty glass on top of its wood surface, while a weathered easy chair waited to one side with a reading lamp nearby. To our right, a stairway stretched up into the shadows of the second floor while a darkened kitchen lay past a narrow door on the other end of the living room.

And that was it. No pictures hung on the walls. Nothing warm or familiar dotted the room. Functional defined the space, as much as it defined the man still watching us. Dressed in a green flannel shirt with faded black cargo pants below it, his only concession to being at home seemed to be the fact wool socks covered his feet instead of the muddy work boots resting to one side of the door. With his graying hair pulled back in a rough ponytail at the nape of his neck and his salt-and-pepper beard reaching from his chin to the top of his chest, he looked like the kind of person who had little need for society, and could probably live quite happily without coming near it for years on end.

"Let me find you some blankets," the man said, keeping an eye to us while he headed for the closet below the stairs. The door squeaked when he tugged it open and, a moment later, he came back with a pair of rough gray blankets in his arms. Handing one to each of us, he waited till we'd wrapped them around our shoulders and then motioned to the couch. "Take a seat. I'll get you some..." He seemed to run a quick inventory in his head. "You drink coffee? I think I have decaf."

"Sure," I said when Zeke paused. "Thank you."

We sat down while he left the room.

"Now what?" I asked softly.

Zeke didn't respond, his gaze on the kitchen. The sound of running water came from farther inside, along with the clink of mugs. A moment later, the steam-puff noise of a coffee maker followed.

The man came back in. "Should just be a few minutes." He crossed the room to his easy chair and sat down on the edge of it. Bracing his elbows on his knees, he folded his hands and regarded us both.

"You all from around here?" he asked finally.

Zeke shook his head. "Just on vacation."

The man nodded. "Well, like I said, I don't have a phone. No good getting cell signal out here, and the landline went down in a storm a few weeks back. Nearest place to make a call is down at the gas station about ten miles away." He glanced to the window as if he could see past the curtains to the rain. "Not smart to be out driving in this weather, though."

I kept my gaze from going to Zeke worriedly.

"I guess you all could crash here for the night, if that's what you'd like?" the man offered cautiously. "I got a room upstairs you could use."

Zeke paused and then looked to me, considering. "That'd work. Thanks."

The coffee maker quieted in the next room. Still studying us, the man made no move to go retrieve the drinks.

I shifted uncomfortably at the scrutiny, my scale swimsuit feeling little better than bare skin beneath the scratchy blanket. "Would you happen to have, like, sweatpants or something I could borrow?" I prompted, pulling the fabric around me tighter.

He gave a slow shrug. "I don't know as anything'll fit you, but I can see what I got."

His gaze stayed on me a heartbeat longer than Zeke, and then he drew a breath, pushing to his feet. He headed into the kitchen.

Zeke watched him go.

"We're staying here?" I asked in a low voice. "We could walk to the gas station."

Not taking his eyes from the doorway, Zeke's mouth tightened. "You haven't slept in a week," he whispered. "Whether or not you reach Kansas, you're still going to need every bit of strength you've got to travel far enough from the water that those bastards can't find you."

I hesitated as dishes clinked in the kitchen. I knew he was

right. I hadn't wanted to sleep, though. Not when every time I closed my eyes, memories returned of a blindfold closing over my head and people punching me in the darkness. Even thinking about it now made me shiver. But at the same time, I knew that, stranger's house or not, if I closed my eyes I'd probably pass out where I sat. And it could be hours more till we found someone else to help us.

"Okay, but–"

I paused as the man came back into the room, a pair of mugs in his huge hands. Murmuring our thanks, we both took them.

The bitter decaf spread through me, warm and relaxing despite the lack of sugar or cream. Wrapping my fingers around the ceramic sides of the plain mug, I watched the man while he headed upstairs.

"You sleep," Zeke said. "I'll keep an eye out, alright?"

I glanced to him. "Okay."

He nodded, not quite looking at me. He took a sip from the mug and then grimaced at the taste and returned the cup to the table.

Silence fell while I finished my coffee. Everything felt awkward around him, and not just because of the strange surroundings or the fact his brother was a Sylphaen.

I still wasn't quite sure what to do with myself, with him so close. With what had happened between us in the cave still hanging in the air.

Footsteps clomped on the steps as the man came back

down to the living room.

"Got you some stuff that might fit," he said, his arms full of a mismatched bundle of clothes. "Though you, uh…"

He paused. "What're your names?"

I swallowed. "Chloe."

"Zeke."

The man nodded thoughtfully. "Earl," he offered. "So yeah, stuff might be kind of big on Chloe. It belonged to my girl. She, uh, she was a bit larger than you."

His face tightened for a moment, something almost like anger flashing over his face, but before I could catch more than a glimpse of the expression, he covered it by turning away to set the clothes on the easy chair. Leaving the pile on the seat, he turned and headed to the kitchen without another word.

I hesitated and then stood, leaving the rough blanket on the couch. From the pile, I drew out a pair of jeans. Checking the tag inside, I saw they were a size or so above my own, but when I pulled them on, they weren't so large as to be unwearable. A forest green tank top followed and I shifted around uncomfortably at the feeling of both it and the jeans on my scales.

Once I had a chance to do so without raising suspicion, I'd really have to change my skin further.

Earl came back in. He paused at the sight of me, his face tightening again, and I dropped my gaze away. I didn't know what'd happened to his daughter, but it didn't take a genius to see it wasn't something good.

"Thank you for the clothes," I said as Zeke rose and retrieved a shirt from the pile.

Earl nodded and continued into the room. He took my mug from the table and then hesitated briefly when he noticed Zeke's cup was still full. Not saying a word, he picked up both and returned to the kitchen.

I sighed, exhaustion stealing over me as he left. The mere feeling of clothes brought back how long it'd been since I'd stayed on land for any length of time, and everything that'd happened between then and now.

Not the least of which was truly how little I'd slept.

I walked to the couch and sat down.

Zeke glanced back at me. "You okay?"

I nodded. "Just... yeah, tired."

He watched me for a moment. "Hey, Earl?"

The man leaned his head out of the kitchen.

"That room you were talking about," Zeke prompted. "You think you could show that to us?"

Earl nodded, and then jerked his head toward the stairs. Following his own direction, he walked over to the steps.

I pushed away from the couch, though my limbs didn't seem to want to support the motion. Seeing me wobble, Zeke came over and took my arm. I started to protest the help even though his touch felt as warm and amazing as ever, but nothing seemed to respond, including my words.

I'd never been this tired in my life.

Together we crossed the room and climbed the steps, Earl going ahead of us. At the landing, he turned and walked through an open doorway just beyond the staircase.

Zeke led me inside. A queen-size bed waited to the left, covered in blankets not much different than the rough one I'd left downstairs. Twin windows flanked it, each of them partially shielded by ratty curtains and sunken into the wall with window seats on their bottom edges. A dresser stood at the far end of the room, its top as bare as the rest of the space.

I clung to Zeke while he continued toward the bed, my legs feeling heavier with every step. I lay down, not even bothering to pull back the rough blanket, and my eyes closed immediately when my head touched the pillow.

"You want something else to drink?" I heard Earl ask. "Not coffee?"

Zeke hesitated. "Sure. Thanks."

My brow furrowed. Something felt wrong about that. About all of this. I couldn't believe I was so tired.

And then sleep claimed me.

"…do it in Jeri's old room."

Earl's words filtered through the cotton stuffing in my head, barely making sense.

"Yeah, well, seemed fitting." He paused. "Listen, Richard, I called you as a courtesy, on account of how you said one got away from you yesterday. But it took me an hour after the girl collapsed to get the boy to finally conk out, and with that damn scum-sucker metabolism of theirs, you know I can't promise either of 'em will be down for long. You and your boys want any part of this, you better hurry up and get here."

Alarm struggled through me, weighed down by an exhaustion that wanted to smother my mind back into sleep. Scumsucker? He…

"Hang on," Earl said as though interrupting someone. "One of them ain't breathing the same as they were."

My heart began to pound harder while I fought to open my eyes. Breathing? He sounded so far away. How could he hear anyone *breathing*?

Footsteps clunked on the hardwood floor. Light pierced the blackness around me as I managed to lift my eyelids. I was on the bed, facing the doorway. In the window seat, Zeke was slumped, his head resting on the wall. The room was dark around us, though the hall light was on.

Earl came to the door. In one hand, he held a phone to his ear, and at the sight of me, he made an angry noise.

"What'd I tell you? The girl's awake."

He dropped the phone onto the window seat as he strode toward me, and all my dull commands to my muscles couldn't make my body move. Striding past me, he retrieved something from the dresser and then returned with a sports bottle in his hand.

I tried to pull away, but he just reached down and grabbed

my head from behind, lifting it toward him. With his teeth, he popped open the top of the bottle and then shoved it into my mouth.

Bitter-tasting liquid flooded my throat. I choked, the drink spewing from my lips, but he just dropped the bottle and clamped an enormous hand over the lower half of my face.

"Swallow," he ordered.

I stared up at him. His grip tightened on my hair, tugging at my scalp.

"Now."

Someone shouted angrily from the tiny speaker of the cordless phone, their words indecipherable. Earl's face darkened and he glanced to the window seat.

Spikes crept from my forearms, finally answering the frantic signals from my brain. As he turned back toward me, I flopped my arm out like the dead weight it was, succeeding in catching his side.

With a pained cry, he lurched away, his hand leaving my mouth.

I spit the liquid out and struggled backward, half-crawling and half-tumbling from the opposite side of the bed.

"Zeke," I croaked.

He didn't move.

Earl made a furious noise while he straightened, clutching at his side. Blood darkened his flannel shirt.

But he didn't look startled. He didn't look surprised in the least by the tips of the iridescent knives protruding from my skin.

"What..." I tried. "Why are you..."

He glanced from me to Zeke, and then to the phone still laying on the window seat. Annoyance twisted his face. He reached over, retrieving the bottle from the floor, and then he returned his gaze to me.

Clutching the edge of the bed, I trembled. "Please. I'm not your enemy."

"Tell that to my daughter."

My brow furrowed.

He started around the bed. I scuttled backward, my legs still refusing to hold me, though the spikes listened and grew longer. Half-sprawled on the floor with my back to the wall, I lifted one of my arms in front of me like a shield.

Earl stopped.

"I don't..." I managed, breathing hard with the effort of keeping my arm up. "I don't know your daughter. Please."

A snarl curled across his mouth. "Please," he repeated scornfully.

He kicked my legs, toppling me sideways. His hand came down on my wrist, avoiding the spikes, and he twisted it. I shrieked as pain shot through my arm. Dropping the bottle from his other hand, he took my throat.

"Stab me again and I break your neck right now," he growled.

Not waiting for a response, he shifted his grip from my throat to my other wrist and then yanked me with him. Like a flour sack, he dragged me from behind the bed and started across the room.

"'Please'," he muttered as he went. "That's what you all come down to. You and your magic. Begging. You know she begged me too? My own girl. Begged me to kill her after what that scaly bastard did. After I finished him off. Said she couldn't live without him." He scoffed. "*Him*. First scum-sucker she'd found, and one she'd already started gutting like the fish he was. But then he got his hands on her and…"

Earl looked down at me. "You try any of that make-me-love-you shit on me, I'll be sure I remember just enough to kill your boyfriend nice and slow right in front of you, got it?"

I stared up at him, screaming in my head for my limbs to move. For anything to start working. My arms were going numb from the angle at which he was holding them, and nothing in my body seemed to want to work right.

My gaze went to the window seat. "Zeke!" I cried. "Zeke, wake up!"

His brow furrowed, but he didn't open his eyes.

And then Earl pulled me into the hallway.

Hardwood slid beneath my back and my legs bumped into the oak railings lining the stairwell. The light overhead glared in my eyes as we passed below it, and then Earl turned, hauling me into the shadows of another room.

My vision sharpened out of desperation when he shut the door. Painted shelves hung on the walls, with figurines of ballerinas and horses on them. Faded posters were taped nearby,

17

featuring Hollywood stars and pop bands that had been famous nearly two decades ago. Everything was covered in a thick layer of dust, as though it hadn't been touched in years.

Something like stiff fabric bunched up at my shoulders with a crinkling sound. Shifting his grip, Earl heaved me upward and then dropped me to the floor again.

I rolled my head to the side awkwardly. Plastic. I was lying on sheet plastic.

Heart pounding, I tried to push away from the ground, but my arms just tingled with numbness and wouldn't hold my weight. I struggled to roll over, my gaze searching for Earl.

He was standing at a white-painted vanity, with a four-post bed covered in teddy bears and a white quilt nearby. Pink ribbons hung from the edges of the mirror, while an old strip of pictures like those taken at an amusement park photo booth was tucked into the space between the glass and its frame. Swiftly, my eyes picked out the details. Earl, though his beard was shorter and he was smiling, and at his side, a round-faced girl of maybe fourteen or fifteen with curly brown hair and an embarrassed expression that didn't fully hide her grin.

Drawing a breath, he lifted a hand to the photos. In the reflection of the mirror, I could see his eyes close, pain and rage on his face in equal measure.

I shoved at the floor, succeeding in moving a few inches backward on the cold plastic. But my legs were still dead. Reaching down with one hand and not taking my attention from Earl, I rubbed at them frantically, trying to wake my muscles.

"Jeri was so good with a knife," Earl murmured without opening his eyes. "I taught her since she was practically a baby and she was always so good."

He exhaled sharply, as though pushing the memories aside, and he glanced back at me. "I found her in here, you know? Right about where you're lying. After she'd…"

A shudder ran through him. He returned his gaze to the vanity and then he lifted a large hunting knife from its top.

In my head, I shouted for my legs to move, while spikes stood out from below my elbows to my wrists.

"She was right, though. She always kept my spirits up with her belief you scale-skins were still out there somewhere. And she was right."

He turned, the enormous knife gripped in his fist.

Adrenaline made its way to my legs. Shoving awkwardly from the plastic, I scrambled toward the closed door, not taking my eyes from him. My hand fumbled for the handle.

The door was locked.

"You know the wonderful thing about your kind?" he commented, watching me. "You don't exist. So no cops'll come looking when you disappear."

He strode toward me, the plastic crinkling beneath his feet. I felt desperately around the knob, trying to find the lock.

My fingers landed on it. Frantically, I turned it and then grasped at the knob again.

He lunged at me.

I dropped to the ground as the knife slammed into the white wood above my head. Swinging out frantically, I slashed at his leg, and he jumped back, narrowly avoiding the spikes. I twisted, reaching for the handle.

His hands grabbed me under my arms. With a snarl, he heaved me away from the door and flung me onto the plastic sheet.

I landed hard, the air rushing from my chest while stars burst across my vision. Gasping with pain, I blinked, trying to make my sight clear as I looked toward the door.

With a furious jerk, Earl yanked the blade from the wood and then turned to me.

His eyes flared red. Fissures radiated across his face, glowing like fire burned inside and spreading farther down his skin.

I stared, a whole new version of terror rushing through me as he started across the room. My hands pushed at the floor, my sweaty palms slipping on the plastic sheeting and my body protesting the motion. I retreated till the four-post bed brought me up short.

Earl smirked. His fingers adjusted on the hilt of the hunting knife.

Grabbing at the dusty quilt, I pulled myself upright, not taking my eyes from him. The faint moonlight beyond the windows caught on the blade of his knife, and beneath his feet, the crinkling of the plastic sounded as loud as the rapid pounding of my heart.

The door swung open. Earl paused, looking back.

Zeke stood in the hall, one arm bracing him on the door-frame. His face was haggard, and he breathed hard with the effort of keeping his feet, but rage colored his skin as he glared at Earl.

"Get... the hell... away from her," Zeke growled.

Earl scoffed. With a quick motion, he hurled the knife through the doorway.

Zeke dropped to the floor as the knife flew past him to impale itself in the wall on the far side of the stairwell.

My gaze darted from Zeke to him. I lunged forward and drove my spikes into the enormous man.

Or tried to.

It felt like hitting a wall of rock. Pain reverberated through my arm, while the blades barely penetrated his side.

Earl looked back at me, disgust curling his lip.

His hand grabbed my throat.

I choked as the pressure of blood unable to escape filled my head. My fingers clawed at his grip and blackness flooded the edges of my vision. I couldn't breathe, couldn't scream, and my hands tearing at his might as well have been trying to bend stone.

By the doorway, I saw Zeke push back to his feet and charge at Earl.

The huge man seemed to hear him coming. Still gripping my neck, he twisted, his other hand catching Zeke.

With an inhuman roar, he threw Zeke backward, propelling

him into the oak railing lining the stairwell. My heart froze as Zeke clutched at the wood, barely stopping himself from going over the side.

And then Earl turned back to me. His hand tightened on my neck and heat like a furnace poured from the cracks still spreading down his arm toward me.

"For my daughter," he snarled.

I looked up at him. The pounding in my head was excruciating. Shadows were devouring the world. Nothing I could do would break his hold.

My hand clutched his and with everything I had, I willed him to give a damn about me. To love me. Care. Anything.

A shiver like electricity raced through my body, overriding the pressure in my head and the pain.

Earl stumbled and gasped, releasing me.

I crumpled to the ground while he staggered backward. Coughing, I pressed my palms to the slats of the hardwood floor, just trying to stop the world from spinning.

"What..." he stammered. "What'd you..."

My throat burned with every breath and my stomach roiled. I looked over at him, finding him staring down at me with confusion and fury waging an all-out war on his face.

"You... you *bitch*!" A shudder ran through him and he made a choked sound, as though his body rebelled at the word. "I..."

With a shaking hand, I grabbed at the side of the bed and dragged myself up. The world bucked and my legs wobbled as though neither of them wanted to hold me. Through the open doorway, I could see Zeke pulling himself back upright as well.

"Get away," I rasped at Earl, and another shiver tingled through me, as if the aveluria magic affected my words as well.

The man shuddered again, his feet moving backward though the hatred on his face just increased. Gritting his teeth, he came to a stop and then shook his head, as if struggling to drive something from his mind.

His foot lurched forward.

"No," I tried, every sound hurting. "S-stay back…"

He retreated a step. A cry escaped him, the noise somewhere between rage and anguish. Desperation twisted his face while his gaze skittered across the room, coming to rest on his daughter's picture against the mirror.

A growl rumbled in his chest, growing louder. His body went rigid and his fists clenched. Fissures spread through his skin as though driven by an earthquake.

I shoved away from the bed. In a stumbling run, I bolted around him toward the door.

His hand swung through the air, grabbing at me and narrowly missing. With a snarl, he staggered after me.

Zeke caught me and pulled me with him from the doorway. Shoving me ahead of him, we ran for the stairs.

Earl was right behind us.

We reached the landing. My hand clutched the railing as

we whipped around the turn.

Earl snagged Zeke's shirt. With a roar, he yanked him backward and then drove Zeke through the open doorway of the room he'd shown us hours before.

Red eyes glowing, he turned to me.

"No," I gasped. "No, stay–"

My back bumped into the wall. My hands plastered to it while I inched to the side, attempting to get away from the gaping opening of the stairwell.

A grimace of effort contorting his face, Earl reached for me.

Zeke slammed into him. I ducked as Earl staggered against the wall above me and then twisted to grab Zeke again.

I lunged and shoved him hard.

Earl stumbled sideways. His foot hit the top stair and slipped. Lurching backward, he fought for balance and his hands grabbed at the banister.

He missed.

The ground shook as he crashed down the stairs.

And then the house was still.

My eyes locked on the stairwell. I barely breathed. Trembling, I tugged my gaze to Zeke. He looked like the hand bracing him on the railing was the only thing keeping him standing. Swallowing hard, I crept to the top of the staircase.

Earl lay on his side at the base of the steps, his arm pinned under him and his legs still sprawled on the stairs. On his skin, the cracks had mostly faded. His eyes were closed. But for the slow movement of his chest beneath his green flannel shirt, he showed no sign of life.

"Come on," Zeke said, moving past me and cautiously descending the stairs.

I followed, not taking my eyes from Earl. We reached the first floor and, heart pounding, I stepped past the man, waiting for him to wake and grab at me again.

He didn't move. The rain pouring down like water from a hose was the only sound.

I drew a breath, trying to keep myself from shaking while I looked around the living room. We needed to get out of here. He'd been talking to someone else on the phone. Someone like him, who wanted to hurt us.

Someone who, from the sound of it, could be on their way here right now.

The shaking got worse. With a trembling hand, I ran my fingers through the rat's nest tangle of my hair.

My gaze landed on his car keys on the table beside the door. I froze, shivers running through me for a whole other reason.

I looked over at Zeke to find him regarding the keys too.

He met my eyes, and from his expression, he seemed to have the same thought as me. "You drive?"

I nodded.

He went for the keys.

My heart still racing, I looked back at Earl. At the wallet in his pocket.

We'd need money. We'd need gas and maybe food.

I couldn't believe myself. My life. Any of this.

Barely daring to breathe, I approached him. He didn't move when I crouched down, as far from him as I could be while still keeping him in reach. Gingerly, I drew the wallet from his back pocket.

He groaned.

My heart scrambled up my throat. Straightening as fast as my muscles could move, I backpedaled from him and retreated to Zeke's side. His eyes fastened on the man, Zeke pulled open the door.

We headed outside.

The night beyond the porch was pitch black and rain gushed down in a torrent. With legs that felt like rubber, I jogged across the sodden yard toward the truck, with Zeke coming behind. The doors weren't locked, and when we pulled them open, the smell of dust and old motor oil filtered into the rainy night air.

We climbed in, the musty bench seat squeaking loudly beneath us. The engine growled when it kicked over, and the gearshift by the steering wheel locked into reverse at my frantic tug.

The front door opened again and light from the house spilled into the yard. One arm hanging awkwardly at his side and the other bracing him on the wall, Earl gave a furious shout at the sight of us in his truck.

He started down the stairs.

I flattened the pedal to the floor and sent the truck flying backward. Crushing my bare foot to the brake, I took only long enough to throw the gearshift into drive and crank the wheel in a turn, and then we were off again.

The truck raced down the dark road, carrying us away from Earl.

2

ZEKE

I didn't know where we were going and I was fairly certain Chloe didn't either.

Though I doubted either of us cared.

My ribs ached from hitting the rails beside the stairs and my body felt like it'd been run over by the rig of a deep sea trawler. For her own part, Chloe looked like she'd gone a dozen rounds with a giant squid and barely survived. From the darkening skin around her neck to the marks I'd spotted on her shoulders and arms, there didn't seem to be an inch of her that wasn't banged up somehow.

I hated the sight of it and my stomach roiled at the thought of what that bastard had been about to do to her. In all of dehaian history, I'd never heard of anything like the monsters we'd encountered in the past day. But between that Noah guy and now Earl, I was starting to wonder how many people over the years who I'd thought were human had actually been those greliaran things in disguise.

Another wave of dizziness rolled through me and I rested my head against the cold glass of the window, waiting for it to pass. That psycho had given us something, and that something was taking a damnably long time to wear off.

"You okay?" Chloe asked over the roar of the rain.

I looked over. In brief twitches, she pulled her gaze from the road to glance at me worriedly. With effort, I buried a grimace. "Yeah," I replied, straightening again. "You?"

She nodded. Her hands adjusted their death grip on the steering wheel while she returned her focus to the track ahead. The twin lights of the truck illuminated the narrow gravel path, though the night swallowed the forest on every other side. With an emerald sheen, her green eyes glowed, obviously compensating for the darkness.

I watched her, not believing the silent answer for a moment.

But from the way she shuddered every few seconds, I also got the feeling that pushing her was a really bad idea right now.

The track widened and the truck bounced over holes in the gravel surface. The line of trees pulled farther back, giving the rain more opportunity to pound down and turn the grassy ditches on either side of the road to deep water and mud. In misleading curves that felt more maliciously random than anything, the road twisted, heading first away from the ocean and then gradually toward it again.

But no signs appeared. Nothing showed where we were,

not even the invisible stars overhead.

Lights glared as a maroon SUV raced around the turn ahead. Chloe hissed with pain, wincing while she quickly adjusted her eyes back to normal human sight. The SUV flew by, passing only inches from the truck's side.

Red light flashed behind us. I twisted in the seat in time to see the vehicle come to a sharp stop.

Chloe muttered a desperate curse.

"What?" I asked.

"When I woke up, I heard Earl calling someone. They sounded like they might be the same as him."

Trying not to swear as well, I looked back at the SUV. It was turning around. Inside, I could see the shadowy forms of five people so big, it was hard to believe they'd fit in the vehicle.

And then the SUV's rear tires hit the side of the road. Hit the mud and the water, and the vehicle lurched down. For a heartbeat, the SUV stopped, and then the other tires spun on the slick gravel and the vehicle rocked, as though trying to drag itself from the mud.

"They're stuck," I told her. "Go!"

The truck accelerated as Chloe pushed the pedal farther toward the floor. A curve in the road swallowed my view of the SUV.

Chloe kept going. Small sounds escaped her while the tires slid, barely keeping to the wet road. A triangular sign bearing the word 'yield' flashed past as the road curved again and joined a broader strip of concrete. With a quick glance over her shoulder, Chloe raced the truck through the turn, sending it skidding onto the highway ahead of a semi.

Angry honking followed us as we sped away.

"Anything?" Chloe asked.

I looked back. "No."

A breath left her. On the wheel, her hands shook and she adjusted her grip distractedly.

"Chloe," I tried.

She didn't respond. Breathing hard, she tossed short glances to the mirror, checking the road, and then steered the truck around another semi in our path.

I returned my gaze to the highway. I wanted to reach out and take her hand. I wanted to do something, anything to calm her. But I wasn't sure it'd be welcome. In fact, I was pretty certain it wouldn't, given how tense things had been between us for the past day. At best, I'd just upset her more. At worst, I'd startle her enough to accidentally send the truck careening from the road.

And so I did nothing and hated myself for it.

Life had never been as complicated as it had become in the past few weeks. Hell, the past few days alone were more complicated than anything else combined. We'd managed to survive that behemoth, and an attack by mercenaries before that.

And my brother.

I closed my eyes, drawing a breath to steady myself. I still didn't know what to think about that. How to feel. Niall had joined the Sylphaen. He'd killed our dad, or at least agreed to let it happen, and nearly killed our older brother Ren as well. He'd lied to me, to Ina, to all of us for years, and never once gave any sign he'd thrown his loyalty in with those psychopaths.

And a few hours ago, he'd kidnapped Chloe with the intent of killing her to somehow gain abilities he claimed she possessed.

I didn't know what to believe anymore. I was just so angry I felt like taking on a shark.

Or fifty.

Opening my eyes, I locked my attention on the terrain while I tried to calm down. I'd deal with Niall. Fix this somehow. I'd make it so that Chloe really could be safe in Nyciena, and my sister and Ren too, and get the Sylphaen away from us once and for all. The woman Niall had worked with, Liana, was already gone. I'd killed her – an act I knew I should feel... something... about, even if I couldn't figure out what. And the rest of them would be stopped. I'd get back home and I'd make Ren understand that had to happen.

But later. It would have to come later. At the moment, the ocean was still full of those bastards. I needed to get Chloe away from here.

Even if I had no clue where 'here' was.

I scanned the landscape beyond the road. The rain had slowed over the past few minutes, becoming nothing more than a light drizzle. Moonlight pushed past the thinning cloud cover, silvering the trees and the wide fields that interrupted them. In the shadows, enormous houses nestled on the far sides of the open spaces, darkened for the night with only the occasional security light to draw attention to their presence.

It all felt surreal, and not just because I'd never ridden in a truck, or even a car, before. The sensation of flying over the ground without moving a muscle was incredible, to be sure. But I'd never traveled so far from the ocean that the air didn't carry its salty smell and gaps in the terrain didn't show glimpses of the water. It was so strange.

And it was starting to become uncomfortable.

I swallowed as a prickling sensation ran over my skin. We were crossing more than a mile a minute, if the markers by the roadside were any indication. It wouldn't be long till the discomfort became so strong, I couldn't go any farther.

Fighting back a grimace, I shifted on the seat. That was the point. When I reached the limit of how far I could go, any Sylphaen would have too. And that'd mean Chloe was safe.

Though there were still the behemoths we'd left in the SUV to consider.

And maybe they couldn't travel far from the ocean either. Or maybe they wouldn't be able to track her, now that we'd left them stuck on that little country road. The point was, the more distance she had from this place, the more she'd stand a chance of escaping the people who'd tried to hurt her.

Of course, she'd also be alone.

The prickling on my skin increased. I couldn't help that. I

could only get her as far from here as possible and then head back to deal with Niall. He'd sworn he wouldn't touch Ina, and I'd warned her about him besides, but he'd also been lying for damn near half a decade.

I couldn't risk him hurting my sister.

And I didn't want to leave Chloe by herself, miles from her home.

My brow furrowed as I pushed the last thought away. What I wanted didn't matter. The ocean and the fact I was dehaian wasn't going to give me a choice.

Light glowed against the night sky while we descended toward a city and then gradually followed the curving highway around its edge. The miles sped past, and time did too, and soon the night swallowed the city again.

I felt like someone was running razors over my skin.

Shivering, I adjusted my position on the seat. Just a bit farther, and I'd tell her we needed to stop. That she had to go on alone.

A mile flew by. The razors dug deeper, bit into my muscles and bones, and tugged like a thousand fishhooks trying to drag me back toward the sea. A short gasp escaped me at the pain and involuntarily, my hand twitched for the door handle.

"Zeke?" Chloe called worriedly.

I couldn't move to look at her and my voice felt lodged in my throat. I pulled a ragged breath through gritted teeth, trying to find a way to speak.

"Oh God, Zeke!" she cried. "I'm so sorry! I wasn't even–"

She steered the car to the side of the highway and came to a quick stop. Twisting on the bench seat, she grabbed my hands.

A feeling like the ocean itself spread from my fingers and up through my arms, driving the pain away. Blinking, I looked over at her.

"What?" she asked, confused by my expression.

"What did you do?"

Her head shook. "Nothing."

I stared at her while the feeling of razors and fishhooks melted away as though it'd never been. "You made it stop. The pull of the water."

Chloe's brow furrowed in desperate bafflement. "I-I didn't... I was just worried."

Her gaze dropped to our hands. Swallowing hard, she inched her fingers from mine.

The pain didn't return.

"Are you still okay?" she asked.

I nodded.

She echoed the motion, seeming shaken. Drawing an unsteady breath, she put her hands back on the steering wheel and glanced to the highway.

"Chloe?"

A semi flew past, its lights silhouetting her briefly before it was gone.

"Bit farther then?" she asked without turning back to me.

I hesitated. "Yeah."

She nodded again. The truck pulled onto the road.

I watched her as a minute crept by. Her hands flexed on the steering wheel every few moments and her face looked like she was keeping herself calm by willpower alone.

"How *are* you going to get back?" she asked quietly.

"Figured I'd walk. Maybe hitchhike."

She paused. "That's pretty dangerous."

"I'll be fine."

Another moment passed.

"We probably should stop soon then," she said, her eyes still on the road and her voice small.

I didn't respond. I needed to get back to protect Ina. I didn't want to leave Chloe alone.

"Zeke?"

"Not yet."

Her gaze twitched to me questioningly. "But, if you're going to make it back safely–"

"Not yet."

She hesitated and then gave a tiny nod.

The truck continued down the highway to the glow of lights from passing cars and the growl of the tires over the concrete.

One of her hands left the steering wheel and reached over to me. Her fingers wrapped around mine, gripping them tightly, and I could feel her trembling.

Fields swept by, with distant houses picked out by security lights like land-bound stars.

"Are *you* okay?" I asked carefully.

Her eyes didn't leave the road. "Fine."

I put my other hand on top of hers. I felt her tense.

"We probably should still stop at some point. Just to rest for a bit."

She shook her head. "I'm alright."

I paused. "Yeah," I agreed, though I suspected that wasn't remotely true. "But you still need to sleep eventually."

Her hand quivered in mine.

"Chloe."

An exit sign flew past, and its corresponding road too. I saw her gaze flick toward it and then back to the road.

I let out a breath, uncertain what to do. She couldn't keep going like this. Not all the way back to Kansas, however far away that was.

"There's nowhere to stop," she argued, a touch desperately. "Hotels will probably want ID and we don't–"

"Just pull over somewhere. Away from the highway."

She stopped herself from glancing to me and kept driving.

A mile passed, and then several more. Another exit sign came into view and in the distance, I could see reflectors marking where its road began. The night swallowed everything else, and the country highway the exit led to showed no signs of civilization along it for miles.

"Please, Chloe."

She shivered.

My hand tightened on hers.

She guided the truck onto the exit road.

I didn't say anything while we continued on, leaving the

interstate in the darkness behind us. At the tiny intersection of a gravel road, she turned again, and when the highway had vanished from view, she pulled the truck from the path and came to a stop.

She lowered her hand from the steering wheel.

"Why don't you want to sleep?" I asked her quietly.

A heartbeat passed.

"Brings it back," she whispered.

My brow furrowed. "Brings what back?"

"What they did. Locking me up. The blindfold. The…"

She shifted her shoulders as though trying to get away from something.

Memory filled in the blanks. Even before Earl had attempted to kill us, there'd been the Sylphaen. That bitch, Liana, and her people who'd beaten Chloe when they dragged her from the pit Ren had put her in.

I took a careful breath, fighting to keep my anger at them from my tone. "I understand."

Her gaze flicked toward me, not meeting my eyes.

"But," I continued, "this is hurting you too."

Her brow twitched down.

"You're safe, Chloe. They're not going to find us. The Sylphaen can't even come inland this far."

She looked up at me, her green eyes glowing faintly in the darkness.

"You're safe," I said again. "You…"

I hesitated and then reached over, unbuckling the seat belt

holding her. I knew what I wanted to do. I just didn't know if she'd let me.

"You can sleep," I told her. "I'll stay awake. I'll... I'll keep the memories away."

Beneath my hand, I felt her tremble. For a moment, she hesitated, and then she inched across the seat toward me.

Gently, I pulled her closer, a breath leaving me at finally having her in my arms again. I could feel her shaking when she laid her head on my shoulder, and carefully, I lifted my hand, brushing the auburn waves of her hair from her cheek.

"Just sleep," I whispered as she closed her eyes. "It's going to be okay."

3

CHLOE

I opened my eyes to sunshine pouring through the windows and the warmth of Zeke beside me. We were leaning against the door, his arms held me close, and my hand was on his chest.

A blush raced up my neck. Pushing away from the seat, I looked over at him. "I, um… "

"Good morning," he said into my awkward pause, a smile tugging at his lips.

I hesitated. He didn't appear upset. And why would he? Zeke seemed like he'd wanted what had happened between us so far. I'd been the one to bring it to a stop.

Even if I'd wanted it as well.

I dropped my gaze from his. I'd been too tired last night to argue. Too tired to do more than welcome the chance to avoid the nightmares I'd known were waiting. And he'd felt wonderful, holding me in his arms.

He always felt wonderful.

My face grew hotter. "Morning," I replied, my voice hoarse from the bruises I could feel on my neck. I shifted on the seat to pull away.

"Hey," he said.

I froze.

"What's wrong?"

I shook my head, the motion jerky and totally a lie. "Nothing."

He paused. "Chloe." His brow furrowed when I looked up at him. "Listen, I'm sorry about yesterday. Us. That's not how I wanted..." The furrows deepened. "Well, any of that to be."

"You didn't?" I replied, confused.

He blinked. "No, I-I mean, I wanted that. I just didn't mean to make things so..." he seemed to search for a word, "uncomfortable."

I hesitated, not sure what to say. There was so much more to it than just those few minutes in the cave – amazing, awkward, mistaken, and incredible as they'd been.

"About that..." I began, shifting around to a more upright position on the bench seat.

His eyebrow rose.

"Back in Nyciena." I drew a breath. "Everyone kind of had this idea about, um, us. About how we..."

His curiosity changed to discomfort as he understood. "Ah."

I waited, not quite looking at him.

"Let me guess," he supplied. "Ina said something."

"Not really. It was mostly those Deiliora girls and Count Velior."

"Velior?" he repeated, his voice hardening.

I gave a small shrug.

Zeke looked away, shaking his head to drive the anger from his face. "Sorry. That guy's just such a…"

He trailed off.

"What is it you're after, Zeke?" I asked quietly. "Really? Because they made it sound like you–"

"It's not that," he cut in, his tone harsh.

I was silent.

Zeke took a breath, still not turning back toward me. "I know the reputation I have. I know what some people say. And mostly…" He shook his head. "I'm not going to say they're *right*, but I know what it might look like. But you've got to understand, where I come from this is all a game. Both sides, they know that. They prefer it that way. No one ever wants anything serious, or hardly ever, because they're only after fun and what favors they can get."

He paused. "And then there's you. And you're not like that. You don't care about titles, or what advantage you can gain. With me, you've always just been… you. Even after you knew what and who I was, you didn't change. You were still just you. Beautiful, real, *you*." He gave a soft, incredulous chuckle. "You didn't even *care* that I was a prince."

I tried not to grimace. It wasn't fair to say I hadn't cared. I'd been shocked beyond words. I hadn't known what to–

He seemed to pick up on my discomfort. "Not like the people where I'm from care," he explained gently. "I've never known anyone like that. Not in my entire life. And even though you're fascinating, and incredible, and I've wanted to be with you for, well," the chuckle came again, "a *lot* longer than I let myself know... I think I was afraid that if I got caught up in that or changed how things were between us, I'd just screw everything up." He shook his head. "I didn't want to risk losing what I had with you."

I swallowed, struggling to find words. He could be lying. Could be, except that if he was, his voice and face would put every con artist in history to shame. And then there was the simple question of who to believe. Zeke, who'd repeatedly risked his life to save me. Or a bunch of people I barely knew and couldn't stand anyway.

"I don't either," I whispered.

For a moment, he was silent. His fingers found my own and his head cocked to the side questioningly, his gaze on our hands.

"This isn't going to be the part where you tell me you just want to be friends, is it?" he asked carefully.

His eyes rose to meet mine.

A shiver ran through me. "Do you want it to be?" I replied just as carefully, my heart pounding.

He shook his head. "No."

I hesitated, and then came back toward him.

His hand lifted, taking my cheek, drawing me to him. His

lips pressed to mine, warm, soft and as wonderful as I remembered. Gently, his fingers ran through my hair and down to my neck.

My lips parted, inviting the kiss to deepen.

He didn't hesitate. His tongue slipped between my lips, exploring me even as I explored him. His hands moved down my body, brushing against my breasts and continuing on. My heart raced as his fingers slid beneath my tank top to caress my sides and the small of my back. Tingles quivered through my skin everywhere he touched, like tiny bursts of electricity that felt so amazing it was hard to breathe.

And finally I realized what he'd been doing.

It only took a thought. The shiver of magic left me.

Zeke tensed, his breath catching. His fingers tightened on me and he gave a soft groan.

The magic coming from him intensified.

Time skipped. Stopped. Didn't matter. I wanted more of him. I wanted everything. My mind flashed to the camper-covered back of the truck. To what we could do there, with more room. With the rough, old blankets on the metal floor and how incredible he would feel. His hands on my skin. His hands everywhere. And not just that.

But it scared me too. I'd never been like this with anyone – I'd scarcely even *kissed* a guy before this summer – and as much as I wanted to be with him now, wanted it so much I could scream, I... I didn't know. This was going so fast and I wasn't sure...

His magic faded. His lips broke from mine.

I pulled back and looked at him, unable to keep the uncertainty from my expression. Beneath my hands, I felt his heart pounding, but when his gaze searched my face, I could see understanding come into his eyes.

He reached up, brushing back a strand of my hair.

"It's not just that," he whispered, the words so much softer than they'd been only moments ago.

I trembled. "I-I'm sorry. I–"

His expression became insistent. "Chloe, no. Don't be sorry. Please. I don't want to mess this up, remember? I'm…" A breath left him, the sound almost like a chuckle. "Well, don't get me wrong. I'm more than willing, and whenever you want to…" He smiled and a quiver ran through me at the look in his eyes. "But if you're not comfortable with that right now, it's not worth the risk of ruining this to me. I just want you, Chloe. However you choose to be with me, whatever we do, I just want you."

Hesitantly, I gave a small nod.

He drew me close, kissing me again.

"So," he asked when we parted, "how far is it to Kansas?"

I shrugged. "Maybe a thousand miles or so."

His eyebrow rose and he nodded thoughtfully. "We're not going to just drive straight there from here on out, are we?"

A smile pulled at his lips again as he looked to me askance.

Incredulity bubbled up. "Y-you're going to…"

"Well, I've never seen Kansas," he replied with a casual

shrug.

"But what about Ina and–"

I cut off, not wanting to ruin everything by bringing up Niall.

His flippant expression faded. "I need to make sure you're safe too," he said quietly. "From the Sylphaen and those greliaran things and anything else as well. I know you can take care of yourself – I'm not saying you can't – but I'd still like to try.

"And besides," he continued, and I could hear the hurt in his voice. "Niall's after you. You and Yvaria. Ina's not a threat to that, and Ren…" He took a breath, shaking his head. "I warned her. And Ren will believe Ina long before he'd ever listen to me."

I shifted uncomfortably. "But–"

"Chloe," he interrupted.

I looked back at him.

"This is my choice," he said. "I *will* go back. I'll make Ren understand that the Sylphaen are real even if I have to drag him up to their caves myself. I'm going to fix this so that you can return to the ocean and this…" He twitched his head toward the land around us. "This doesn't have to be forever for you. I'm not going to lose you, Chloe. I won't. But before I leave, I need to know you're someplace safe." He paused. "Please."

I hesitated, wanting to protest even if I couldn't figure out what to say. "Okay…"

Zeke smiled. "Thank you."

"You too."

His smile grew. He leaned closer, kissing me.

"A few more miles, eh?" he suggested when he drew back again.

An answering grin tugged at my lip, though I still wasn't sure I was comfortable with taking him farther from his family.

Even if it was his decision.

Drawing a breath, I nodded and then scooted back to the driver's seat.

The engine grumbled as I turned the key in the ignition. With a growl of tires on the gravel, I pulled the truck out onto the road and headed for the interstate again.

We made it another fifty miles before the gas tank wanted refilling and presented us with the issue of bruises and shoes.

"I never got that," Zeke said. "What's humans' deal with shoes in public places?"

Studying the front door of the gas station, I shrugged. "Disease, maybe? Not getting sued for injuries?"

He made a considering noise.

My mouth tightened as the sliding door rolled back and a rotund man in a cowboy hat walked out. Behind the register, the cashier watched him go, just as he had every other customer in the past ten minutes. He didn't look like the nicest person, with the way he scrutinized everyone as though daring them to steal things or break some rule. Meanwhile, the sticker on the pump next to us demanded that we prepay for any gas, leaving us with little choice but to deal with the clerk.

Even if, after so many days of every other person I'd met wanting to kill me, I would've done almost anything to avoid someone so obviously confrontational.

I sighed. This was the only gas station I'd seen at this exit. I didn't know where the next stop would be. And there did appear to be a display of flip-flops just inside the entrance.

It'd have to do.

I glanced to Zeke and then pushed open the truck door. The hinges protested with a rusty squeak, the noise painfully loud in the relative quiet of the morning. Warm summery air swept around us from the empty field across from the gas station, while the trees near the parking lot rustled with the wind.

Leaving the truck by the gas pump, we walked toward the station door.

"Uh, excuse me," the clerk said the moment the door opened. "You can't come in here like that."

I glued a grin to my face and headed for the rotating stand of flip-flops, my heart pounding.

His narrow face tightened behind his large glasses. "I *said*, you can't come in here like–"

"Hang on," I told him.

Grabbing a pair of flip-flops and leaving Zeke to find

another, I strode up to the register.

"It was this or track all kinds of mud into your store," I lied. "You wouldn't *believe* how messed up we got, trying to push our truck out of a ditch. I hope you don't mind."

I gave him the best smile I could, hoping he didn't comment on the lack of mud on my jeans or the truck outside. Zeke came over, setting his sandals down as well.

The clerk regarded us for a moment. "What happened to you?" he asked, jerking his chin toward the bruises on my neck.

I swallowed, holding onto the smile. "I told you," I said as though it was obvious. "Car trouble."

His mouth curled with annoyance. Snagging the flip-flops from the counter, he contented himself with a glare and then rang them up quickly.

"And eighty bucks of gas for pump six, please," I added, handing him the lone credit card from Earl's stolen wallet.

He glared again. I held my breath, waiting for him to protest the name on the card. But he was too busy eyeing us, and barely glanced to the thing while his fingers smacked the buttons of the register.

"Thanks," I told him, scrawling something on the receipt resembling a signature and then taking the card back swiftly.

We slipped into the flip-flops and then retreated from the store as fast as possible.

"Good grief," Zeke commented.

I made a noise of agreement.

We filled up the gas tank, feeling the eyes of the clerk on us all the while. Not looking back at the store, I climbed into the truck, half-expecting to hear a shout about the stolen card behind me. With a growl of the ancient engine, I started the truck and then pulled away from the station.

A breath left me for what felt like the first time in minutes.

"You okay?" Zeke asked.

I nodded. "Just nervous."

He reached over, taking my hand. "We're doing good."

Making myself continue breathing, I nodded again. I hated that we'd had to use the credit card, despite the fact I knew there wasn't nearly enough cash in Earl's wallet to get us home. I could only hope that, if we saved the cash for later, we'd stand a chance of keeping him from tracking us all the way back to Reidsburg.

Flicking the turn signal, I waited for a car to pass and then pulled onto the onramp. Traffic on the interstate was picking up as the clock on the dash ticked toward midmorning, but as far from big cities as we were, there was still plenty of space for us to merge back onto the highway.

My breath caught and I tensed, sitting up straighter as a semi in front of us moved to the left lane, affording me a view of the cars ahead.

Including the maroon SUV with five huge guys inside.

Zeke glanced from me to the road. "No way," he said, shaking his head incredulously.

Heart pounding, I swept my gaze over the vehicle. The

Washington license plate was familiar. I couldn't remember the exact numbers – it'd been dark and I'd changed my eyes back to mostly human when the vehicle came around the turn – but they still looked like they might be the same. And those gorilla-sized guys, I remembered that.

How the hell could they be here?

I slowed down and changed lanes swiftly to get behind the semi again. With a quick glance to the rearview mirror, I pressed the brake and let the truck's speed drop till cars started swerving around us. Ignoring the angry glares, I scanned the side of the road, praying for an exit.

"How'd they know to follow us here?" Zeke asked.

Wracking my brain, I didn't answer. Minutes crept by until another exit sign finally appeared and, with a quick glance to confirm the maroon SUV hadn't taken the off-ramp as well, I veered across the lanes and sent the truck racing from the highway. At the stop sign at the end of the ramp, I paused, watching the SUV continue down the interstate.

Swallowing hard and trying to stay calm, I took a right. A small town surrounded us, and every passerby who glanced our way made me tense all over again. After an eternity, we reached a gravel road several miles beyond the city limit. I turned the truck down the path, continued for a few moments, and then finally pulled it off onto the grassy shoulder.

Immediately, my gaze went to the rearview mirror.

No one was following us.

My hands shook when I lowered them from the steering

wheel. How had they known? We could have driven anywhere. For that matter, we were dehaian. If they knew what we were – and everything Earl had said made it seem like they did – they'd never think we'd be able to drive this far inland.

It might be unrelated. They might just be on vacation or something.

Nothing in me could be made to believe that.

I twisted in the seat, not satisfied with the view the mirrors were giving me. They had to have learned our plans somehow. In the hours since we left Earl's, they must have–

"Earl," I said.

"What?"

I looked to Zeke, horror moving through me. "We told him. We–"

Letting out a breath, I attempted to slow down. "The greliarans. They can hear like crazy. When I woke up at his house, Earl could tell my breathing had changed from down the hall. And when we were in the living room, before he drugged us–"

Zeke swore. "I said Kansas. When he was in the kitchen, I said Kansas."

I nodded.

He exhaled, grimacing like he was doing a lot more swearing inside his head. And then he paused. "Those middle states are fairly big, though, right? So they won't have any idea beyond that of where we're heading."

"Yeah, but if they're going there, they must have some

kind of a plan."

"Maybe. But do a lot of interstates run there?"

I thought for a moment. "No. Not from the east, anyway. There's really just the one, and then a bunch of smaller roads."

"So maybe they're thinking to catch up with us now, or else wait for us where the highway enters Kansas. They probably figure we don't know they're after us, so we'd take the most direct route."

"Yeah." Another thought occurred to me. "But…"

"What?"

"The credit card. Earl could track it. If he's watching his account, he'll know where we've been. And with this gas guzzler…" I shook my head. "There's a decent amount of cash in that wallet, but definitely not enough to get back on it alone."

Zeke hesitated. "Okay," he allowed. "Then what about this? We leave the main road, but we loop back to it once. Just to use the card, get gas, and make them think we're still on the highway. That'll give us a bit more distance toward your home. Then we leave the interstate for good and use the cash for as long as we can."

I stared at him.

"Dad made us study strategy and tactics growing up," he explained, a touch chagrined.

"Wow."

He shrugged. "So is there someone in your town who would come get us? If we run out of money, I mean."

I tried not to grimace. Baylie might not be back yet. I still didn't know how to explain this whole dehaian thing to her.

And I'd have to face them sooner or later.

"My parents," I said, attempting to keep the reluctance from my voice.

He seemed to hear it anyway. "Would that be alright?"

"It's awkward," I explained. "They're landwalkers. They adopted me. Never told me. Lied to me my whole life."

I cut off, anger boiling up like a wound I'd forgotten about suddenly starting to bleed again.

"Last time I saw them… it didn't go well," I finished.

"You want to do this, then? Go back there?"

I shrugged. "Not much choice, right?"

Zeke paused. "We could come up with another plan."

I looked over at him. It was tempting.

But I couldn't run forever. And he needed to get home too.

"It'll be okay," I said.

A heartbeat passed before he nodded.

Drawing a breath, I put the truck in gear again. "So… not the main route." I glanced to the nameless country road behind us. "We're going to need a map."

In the end, the gas and the money got us within two hundred miles of home before the truck started to sputter.

"So what does that thing say about the nearest town?" I

asked Zeke.

Stabilizing himself while the truck bounced over another pothole in the road, he scrutinized the atlas we'd picked up at a gas station several states ago.

"Corwin, Nebraska. About ten more miles."

I bit my lip. There was little chance we'd make it that far.

Though, considering we hadn't seen a town in what felt like forever, that was still better than nothing.

We continued down the rough highway without a single car in either direction. Fields and flatlands surrounded us, with the occasional farmstead to break the tedium. The mid-morning sky was a brilliant shade of blue with barely a cloud to be seen, while a breeze drifted through the open windows of the truck, breaking the summer heat. We'd driven through the past day and night, stopping every few hours for breaks – wonderful, amazing breaks – while we tracked across state highways and alternate interstates from the one that led straight home.

A choking noise came from the engine. My pressure to the pedal resulted in a short burst of acceleration.

And then nothing.

I pulled the truck over and let it roll to a stop.

A sigh escaped me. I looked to Zeke.

"And now we walk," he said, setting the atlas aside.

I nodded. With a glance to the empty road, I shoved the door open and then climbed from the truck.

Gravel crunched beneath our feet as we headed along the side of the highway.

"So this is the middle of your country," Zeke commented.

I glanced to him. A considering expression on his face, he regarded the fields.

"Bored already?"

He grinned. "No. I'm just… I never thought I'd come here, is all." He shrugged. "It's interesting."

I gave him a wry look.

"I mean it," he protested. "It's… well, it's kind of like home."

My expression became incredulous. "How?"

"Open. Sort of featureless, but still beautiful. And there *is* the big blue expanse overhead."

I scanned the terrain around us. "You're just being nice."

He chuckled. "And?"

I shoved at him jokingly. He caught me and pulled me closer.

His arm around my waist, we kept walking.

"Thank you for coming with me," I said.

"Glad I could."

Past the grassland ahead, a forest came into view, with a town scattered inside it. A water tower rose above the greenery, though if there was a name painted on its side, it wasn't facing us. Two-story houses like faded advertisements from a 1950's magazine lined the street, with cars parked in front of them and a smattering of American flags dotting their yards. At the outer reaches of the town, a gas station sat, a rusting shelter over the pumps and strings of triangular banner flags in red, white and blue looping along its sides.

My brow furrowed, and then I realized that in all the chaos, I'd forgotten that the summer was probably creeping toward the Fourth of July.

With a quick glance in either direction, we crossed the road to the gas station and then walked across the empty lot. A cool blast of air-conditioning hit us when Zeke tugged open the door to the tiny building, most of the windows of which were covered by advertisements for pop and beer.

Behind the register, the twenty-something-year-old clerk glanced up from his gaming magazine. His gaze flicked from us to the empty station lot, and then his brow drew down at the sight of the bruises on us.

"Can I help you?" he asked.

"Um, yeah. Do you have a phone we could use?"

He gave a slow nod. "Sure." He jerked his head toward the other side of the store. "Payphone in the back."

"Thanks. Could you give me some change, then?"

From my pocket, I took out the last of the cash.

He opened the register and handed me quarters for the bills.

I smiled. Turning quickly, I threaded through the aisles with Zeke.

In an awkward little nook at the corner of the store, the payphone clung to the wall. A weathered phonebook had been shoved onto the shelf below it, while barely legible graffiti decorated the walls of its tiny booth. Exhaust from the glass-door refrigerators next to us heated the small space, though their fans provided just enough noise that I could hope that the clerk wouldn't overhear me.

I pulled a few coins from my pocket and sent them clunking into the slot.

My hand trembled as I went to dial.

"Hey," Zeke said quietly. He twined his fingers through mine. "It'll be okay."

I gave a tight nod. My gaze went to the clerk, who was still watching us with a confused expression. Drawing a breath, I returned my focus to the phone and punched in my parents' number.

An electronic message informed me of the charge for the call. I shifted the phone to my shoulder while I dug more of the change from my pocket, not wanting to let go of Zeke's hand, and then sent the coins into the slot.

Moments passed. A digital-sounding ring came from the receiver. Heart pounding, I waited for the call to connect.

"Hello?"

I tensed. "Mom?"

There was a pause. "Chloe?" She made a choked noise. "Chloe! Are you– where are you? Are you okay?"

The genuinely concerned tone in her voice made it hard to breathe, considering how uncommon it was. "Y-yeah, I'm fine. Look, I don't have long. I'm in Corwin, Nebraska. My, um…" I broke off, not wanting to explain about the truck. "I'm kind of stuck here. Could you or Dad come get me?"

"Nebraska?" she repeated.

"Please, I'm running out of change for the phone. We're–"

I caught myself. I didn't want to mention Zeke either. That'd be its own trouble. "I'm at a gas station on the west side of town. Could you pick me up?"

She was silent for a moment. "Yes, we'll be right there."

"Thank you."

A pause followed the words. "Chloe, I..." She cleared her throat, dropping whatever she'd been about to say. "Just... just please stay there."

"Okay."

I waited a heartbeat, but nothing else came. She didn't hang up. Didn't say another word. Uncertain what to do, I hesitated and then returned the receiver to its holder.

"Everything alright?" Zeke asked.

Swallowing hard, I nodded.

"They coming?"

I nodded again.

He reached over, putting his other hand to mine where it still rested on the phone. I blinked and looked up at him.

"What is it?" he asked.

My mouth worked, trying to find the words. "She sounded so... worried. Like, really worried. Not just the stupid fake worry she always has about everything."

His brow furrowed a bit, but he didn't press the topic. "Come on," he said with a glance to the clerk, "let's wait outside."

I followed him from the building. The warm air felt jarring after the ice cold temperature of the station, while the fields and town seemed nearly silent. A trio of parking spots lined the front of the building, with a yellow-painted concrete curb ahead of them. Walking a short distance from the door, we checked that the clerk couldn't see us too well and then sat down.

Birds called to each other. I watched them flitting over the crops across the road.

I couldn't figure out what might have worried her. It couldn't be the Sylphaen. Or greliarans. Or anything else that'd threatened my life in the past week. And surely Noah had mentioned I'd survived changing. I mean, they didn't sound like they'd thought I was dead, and however much of a jerk he'd turned out to be, he still would've had to say *something* when he came back without me.

Right?

"So how long will it take them to get here?" Zeke asked.

I flinched, his voice snapping me from my thoughts. "A few hours, maybe."

A single car sped by on the road. I tensed, struggling not to feel like they might be watching us.

"We have enough change left to get something to eat?"

I glanced to Zeke.

He shrugged. "Couple hours to kill."

I looked back at the cluster of trees called Corwin. Thanks to my weird dehaian metabolism, it'd been a day or so since I'd eaten anything.

And I didn't want to just sit here out in the open the

whole while.

There had to be a restaurant in there somewhere.

"Sure," I agreed.

We stood and headed for town.

∞ 4 ∞

NOAH

"So I was thinking we could get pizza at Deltorio's for dinner. That sound good to you guys? Evening out on the town and all that?"

I looked away from the television as my mom popped her head around the accordion door to the sunken den. With her wavy, blonde hair swinging in her loose ponytail, she waited for our answer.

"Yeah, Sandra," Baylie replied, shifting position in her place at the other end of the long couch. "That'd be great, thanks."

I nodded.

Mom smiled and then she disappeared back down the hall.

Baylie propped her head on her hand and returned her attention to the television. She and I had gotten into town late last night, and we'd been here most of the morning, channel surfing for lack of anything better to do.

"I swear," she sighed as the mid-morning news started, the screen flashing from fuzzy shots of the state capital to reports of some unexpected storm out near Hawai'i. She flipped to a different station. "Cable is so overrated."

My lip twitched as I glanced to her. "Movie marathon?"

"*Please.*"

I pushed away from the couch. Stepping around Baylie's yellow Lab, Daisy, who was asleep in a patch of morning sunlight nearby, I headed for the cabinet below the television. Tugging open the doors, I regarded the rows of movies.

"Comedy... action... what're you thinking?" I offered.

"Whatever you want."

I skimmed the titles in the cabinet. It was a tradition with Baylie and me, watching movies when I came to visit. There wasn't much else to do in Reidsburg, and as activities went, it was a whole lot better than going to the gas station or the other random places people in this small town hung out.

It didn't hurt that we had pretty much the same taste in films, either.

I tugged out a box set of The Godfather movies, and another of the Lord of the Rings. Either would eat most of the day, which wasn't a bad thing. I wanted distractions, and we both needed anything resembling normalcy.

"Thoughts?" I prompted, turning to hold them both up for her.

She blinked, pulling her gaze from the glass patio door. I caught the flash of worry in her eyes, though she buried it fast. "Um, Dad and I watched the Lord of the Rings not too long ago," she replied, her casual tone sounding a bit forced. "So..."

I nodded and turned back to the cabinet, struggling to keep from grimacing. We were right next door to Chloe's old house and the awareness of that fact had sat between us like the elephant in the room ever since we'd gotten into town. We hadn't mentioned it. For my part, I'd barely even looked at the house. I felt guilty for being grateful that we'd avoided the topic, but I really didn't want to think about Chloe. I knew Baylie was worried; no one had explained why Chloe wasn't home, why she'd really had to leave in Santa Lucina, or why, short of one phone call asking for a ride a few days ago, no one but me had heard from her in a week. We'd only said that Chloe had gone away with some family friends for a while, and that she was safe.

But I couldn't figure out how to tell Baylie the truth. Her best friend wasn't human.

And she wouldn't be coming back.

I swallowed, forcing my attention to the movies. We'd done fairly well keeping up the pretense of things being normal. I wasn't about to let that go. Not yet.

"Alright, well, you want to grab the popcorn?" I asked without turning around.

"Yeah, no problem. You want–"

She cut off as a knock came on the front door.

"Hey, Baylie, could you grab that?" Mom called.

Baylie sighed. Rising from the couch, she set the remote down and then walked out of the room.

I put the movies aside. Retrieving the remote from the

coffee table, I scanned the buttons for the one that would switch the input feed away from cable.

Baylie opened the door. I heard her gasp.

And then the sound cut off.

My brow drew down. "Baylie?" I called, dropping the remote to the couch. "Everything alright?"

She didn't respond.

"Where is she?" a familiar voice whispered.

My blood went cold. I ran for the hall.

Uncle Richard stood in the front room. He had Baylie pressed to the wall beside the door, one arm holding her there while his other hand was clamped over her mouth. Wyatt and Brock were just inside, and past them, I could see Owen and Clay watching the neighborhood from the yard.

Their mouths curled into smiles at the sight of me.

"Well, look who's here," Wyatt commented. "Not hiding or anything." He chuckled. "Sloppy, cuz."

My heart raced. Of course I hadn't been hiding – why would I? We were just watching television.

And my psychotic relatives were supposed to be on the coast over sixteen hundred miles away.

I started toward them. Wyatt moved to block me.

"Uh-uh," he cautioned.

"We just want to know where the girl is," Richard said. "No one needs to get hurt here."

Disappointment flashed over Wyatt's face at the words, as though he'd really prefer someone did.

"What girl?" I asked.

His grip tightened on Baylie. Behind his hand, I could hear her give a stifled shriek, her terrified gaze locked on me.

"You know which," Richard said. "Chloe. Where does she live?"

I stared at him. "Chloe? You know she can't be here. She's not–"

"Tell me where she lives, Noah," Richard snapped, the threat in his voice more than clear. "Now."

I shivered, looking from him to Baylie. I couldn't stop all of them. Not before they did something terrible to her.

And I couldn't tell them that Chloe had lived right next door. Even if there was no way she could come back here, not now that she'd become one of the dehaian, there was still her family to worry about.

I didn't want to know how her parents fit into the next step of my relatives' plan.

Swallowing hard, I shook my head. "Just let Baylie go," I said, holding up my hands. Cautiously, I moved down the hallway, watching them all. "You don't need to do this. She–"

"Who was it?" Mom called, coming up the basement stairs.

Richard stepped back, releasing Baylie. She scrambled away from him and around Wyatt, racing to me.

I caught her. Pushing her behind me, I retreated into the front room, not taking my eyes from them.

"Baylie?" Mom continued. "Did you hear what I– Richard?"

I heard her set something down sharply and then come

toward us. Taking one hand from Baylie, I reached out quickly, stopping her.

Mom looked furious. "What the *hell* are you doing here?"

"We just had a question for Baylie and your son, Sandra," Richard replied carefully.

"Ed!" Mom shouted to Baylie's dad upstairs. "I'm calling the police," she continued to Richard, moving away from me toward the phone on the wall. "And you're going to be hearing from our lawyers after what your boys did to Baylie in California, so you–"

"Wyatt!" Richard snapped as the guy started toward her.

I moved fast, getting between them.

Wyatt stopped. The snarl on his face turned to a disgusted sneer when he glanced at me.

Ed's footsteps pounded on the stairs. "What?"

"Peter's brother," Mom snapped. "Came here to 'talk' to Noah and Baylie."

Ed's face went dark. "Get out. You get the hell out of my house right now, you bastard."

He started down the stairs.

"Brock!" Richard barked as his son blocked Ed's path. He looked between Mom and Ed. "Nothing's happened here. Nobody needs to call any cops. We just had a question, and now we're leaving."

His sons looked back at him, incredulity damn near blatant on their faces.

"Go," Richard ordered them, still watching Mom and Ed.

Wyatt and Brock didn't move.

"I said go!"

Brock shuddered and then retreated toward the door.

Wyatt growled. Ed's eyes went wide at the sound.

"Now!" Richard snapped.

Wyatt paused. "This isn't over, cuz," he promised, his voice so low, only Baylie or I stood a chance of hearing. "We're gonna get that bitch. Just you wait."

His gaze slid to Baylie. He winked, a smirk on his face, and then sauntered after his family out the door.

Ed hurried down the steps and slammed the door behind them, throwing the lock the moment it closed. Baylie came back over to me and I put my arms around her, holding her while she trembled.

"Thank you," she whispered.

"You all okay?" Ed asked.

Baylie let out a breath and nodded. Behind me, I heard Mom talking to the local police on the phone.

I didn't take my eyes from the window. Richard and my cousins were climbing into their maroon SUV. Starting the engine fast, Richard cast a look around the neighborhood and then took off down the road.

"What was *wrong* with that boy?" Ed continued. "Did you hear him?"

I glanced to Mom warily as she hung up the phone, wondering how she wanted to handle that.

"Richard's boys have always had problems," she answered

neutrally.

Ed's eyebrows rose and fell. "I'll say."

"That was Chief Reynolds," Mom continued. "He's sending an officer over."

Ed nodded. "You sure you're okay, honey?" he asked Baylie.

"Yeah," she said, trying for a smile. "Yeah, I'm alright."

"You kids just head back to what you were doing," he continued. "We'll keep an eye out here and let you know if the cops need to talk to you, okay?"

Baylie glanced to me and I could read the hesitation in her eyes. "Yeah," she agreed. "Okay."

Letting me go, she started back to the den, her gaze still twitching toward the front window.

I looked to Mom, questioning.

She gave a tiny nod.

Taking a breath, I followed Baylie.

She was waiting for me.

I paused at the door, suddenly wishing I could have stayed out in the living room to help Mom.

Though she probably would've just had questions too.

Cautiously, I took the two steps down into the den and then pulled the door shut behind me.

"What the hell?" Baylie whispered, her quiet voice breaking. "What the *hell*, Noah? They're here? They followed us back *here*? For *Chloe*? What in the—"

She cut off when I looked away. A breath left her.

"What is going on?" she demanded.

"They're crazy."

A scoff escaped her, the sound harsh. "No kidding."

I grimaced as she waited. I couldn't figure it out either. They were insane. Certifiably, utterly, and completely insane. And coming to *Kansas* looking for a *dehaian*? That was a whole new level of madness. No one in their right mind would–

My breathing stopped. No one would. Not unless they knew something I didn't. Not unless they'd seen her, or heard something about her...

She'd lived like a landwalker before she became dehaian. She'd survived when everyone else had sworn her heritage would kill her.

Maybe she *could* come back.

And maybe... maybe I could explain...

I turned to Baylie. "Look, my family is nuts, okay? They... they're fixated on Chloe. But if what they're saying is true," I released a shaky breath, "she might be on her way back here."

Baylie stared at me.

I glanced toward Chloe's house, focusing briefly on suppressing the burning, furious energy inside me that let other greliarans tell where I was. "You stay here," I continued. "Watch for her. I'm going to keep an eye on my cousins, just in case... you know."

Without another word, I headed for the hall.

"But *why* are they fixated on her, Noah?" Baylie cried, struggling to keep her voice down as she followed me. "You said she wasn't like you, but what's this about then? Why do they want to hurt her so much?"

I paused by the den doorway. I didn't have time for this. I needed to get out there. Make sure they didn't find her first. "They just do."

Baylie made an angry noise.

"Please," I insisted. "It's important. Just keep an eye out for her. I'll explain, or, you know, maybe she will once she's safe. But Baylie, these guys..." I exhaled. "They're dangerous. You know that. And the cops... they'll just tell my relatives to stay away or something else useless. There's nothing to arrest them for yet. Not where Chloe's concerned. So please just watch the neighborhood, watch her house, and if there's anywhere else you can think of that she'd go, watch that too. We have to help her."

Baylie stared at me for a heartbeat. "O-okay. I will, but... Sandra and Dad aren't going to let you just stay out there. And what about the cops? What do I tell them?"

I could feel the seconds ticking away. "Tell them... tell them I needed some air." I scowled. That'd only work for a bit. "Or that I'm exploring the area. I'll try to stop back in when I can, just to keep them from getting too weird on you, but otherwise, I'm exploring, eh?"

Despite her worry, she looked skeptical. "Exploring." She drew a breath. "Fine. But the minute Chloe's safe, you're telling me what's going on, understand? I'm done with this secrecy crap."

I nodded.

"And Noah?" she called when I started down the hall.

I glanced back.

"Be careful?"

I hesitated. "Yeah."

I headed for the front door. Reidsburg wasn't huge by any stretch of the imagination, and their SUV wouldn't be too hard to find.

And with any luck, Chloe wouldn't be either. For me, at least.

I drew a breath, trying to calm the hope that choked me at the thought of actually seeing her again.

5

ZEKE

Several hours later found us walking back toward the gas station. We'd finally located a fast food place across town and the handful of change in Chloe's pocket had been enough for us to split a small meal. We hadn't spoken much – just watched the town through the windows – and the same was proving true for our trip back to the station. Biting her lip and jumping every time a car drove by, Chloe appeared utterly distracted.

And nervous as hell.

I slipped a hand around her side, grateful for the freedom to finally hold her and hoping to help her calm down at the same time. She flinched at the slight contact, and then a blush colored her cheeks as her startled expression faded to chagrin.

"Sorry."

I made a dismissive noise.

Her head leaned on my shoulder briefly as she put an arm around me.

"What is it?" I asked.

She shook her head.

I watched her from the corner of my eye, uncertain if I should press her.

"They're crazy," she said, almost as if answering something inside herself. "They've always been crazy."

I hesitated. "Okay."

"I mean, my whole life, it was 'ocean water is diseased', 'rapists live on the beach', all kinds of stuff like that. Even if they *were* trying to keep me from going in the water, that's still an insane way to do it."

She paused, her brow furrowing. Looking up at me, she continued in a smaller voice. "You don't think they thought I was dead or something, right?"

I weighed responses and settled for the most neutral. And honest. "I don't know."

"But Noah… he couldn't have just…" She shook her head, anger filtering across her face, and she sped up, moving away from me. "They *had* to know I was fine. That I'd changed and left with you and all that. He *had* to have told them *that*, at least, so she must've just…"

Chloe trailed off.

"Maybe they were worried you wouldn't come back," I offered quietly.

She stopped, looking back at me, and I couldn't hope to read her expression. "I…"

Her brow furrowed. She turned away again.

Tires rumbled behind us. A breath left her, the sound almost panicked. I glanced over my shoulder.

A green sedan with darkened windows raced around the turn.

"That them?" I asked.

I looked back. Her face was answer enough. Not taking her eyes from the car, she came up beside me.

The sedan veered to the side of the highway and then skidded to a stop in a cloud of gravel dust. A woman climbed out before the man at the wheel had even succeeded in shutting off the engine. Leaving the door open, she hurried across the gravel toward us, her red-rimmed eyes locked on Chloe with a look somewhere close to stifled terror. Behind her, the man got out too, moving awkwardly as if to keep from jostling the white sling holding one of his arms. As brown-haired and brown-eyed as his wife, he seemed only scarcely less worried, and he never took his gaze from his daughter while he closed the door.

I tried to keep my face expressionless, but it was difficult. I'd said perhaps they were afraid Chloe wouldn't come home.

It looked more like they were afraid their daughter would fall dead where she stood.

"Chloe," the man called as he headed for us. "Are you alright?"

"Yeah," she answered, her voice choked. "Thanks for coming."

"H-how did you make it this far?" her mom asked,

clenching her hands together as though to stop them from shaking. "And who did that to your neck? Are you–"

The woman swallowed hard, her gaze darting from Chloe to me as she seemed to reconsider whatever she'd been about to say.

Chloe hesitated. "I'm fine."

I glanced to her when she left the response at that.

Her mother's brow twitched down, the desire to press for more written all over her.

"Who's your friend?" her dad asked.

Chloe drew a breath. "This is Zeke."

I tensed at the sudden alarm in their eyes.

"The boy who…" Her dad looked between us. "But he…"

"Is dehaian, yeah," Chloe filled in. "Like me."

Their faces were a picture, though of confusion, shock or horror, it was hard to decide. In the time it took her to speak the words, they raced through the expressions, coming at last to a rabid sort of denial that varied only in its intensity.

"Chloe, you are *not*–" her mother began.

"Linda," the man interrupted.

With a choked noise, she turned to him.

"Perhaps we should continue this elsewhere," he suggested, his eyes on me.

Linda nodded. She stepped forward even as her husband did the same, like they were closing ranks around their daughter with the full intent of forcing us apart.

Chloe stiffened. "Zeke's coming too."

They stopped. I saw the arguments forming.

Chloe moved closer to my side, almost putting me between herself and them. Without looking away from them, I reached down, taking her hand.

I could feel her shaking.

Her dad blinked and his gaze ran over me afresh, with a heavy dose of protectiveness and threat in there this time.

Linda just twitched as though restraining herself from snagging Chloe's arm and yanking her away from me. Breathing hard, she seemed to flounder for a moment, and then she made an aborted motion to the sedan.

Sticking to my side, Chloe headed for the car. At the rear passenger door, she climbed in and then scooted to the other seat, leaving me to follow.

I got in and shut the door, feeling her parents' eyes on us the whole time.

"You okay?" I asked her.

She gave a tight nod, watching them walk toward the car.

They sank into their seats and didn't say a word while they closed the doors and then put on their seat belts. Her dad turned on the engine and gave the road a brief glance before pulling back onto the empty highway. In short order, he'd spun the car around, sending us eastward once more.

And no one spoke. The tension in the air was so thick, even breathing felt like it would trigger some kind of explosion. On the edge of the passenger seat, Chloe's mom perched and cast strange, truncated looks back to me for no reason I could determine. Behind the wheel, her dad seemed focused on the road, though I occasionally caught him glancing to his daughter in the rearview mirror.

And Chloe never quite looked at them. She never quite looked at anything. Her gaze darted across the middle distance like a fighter expecting an attack and trying to watch every direction at once.

Corwin fell behind us. Fields swept by and so did time. A sign flashed past, notifying us we were entering Kansas, though otherwise, nothing in the landscape changed.

I wondered if anyone planned on making a sound for the entire trip back to their home.

The sun crept toward the horizon and gradually painted the sky with brilliant colors of pink, purple and gold. Shadows stretched from the tall crops lining the highway, growing darker while the twilight deepened.

In the distance, a town came into view, like another island of trees in the midst of a flatland sea. Bigger than Corwin, but still small by far compared to Santa Lucina, it seemed mostly made up of houses, with scarcely a building taller than two stories to be seen.

I glanced to Chloe, curious if we were finally there.

Her expression answered me. It was definitely Reidsburg. She was watching the town roll toward us with a look somewhere between desperation and that of a convict staring at their prison cell.

Minutes crawled by. As the sun sank over the horizon

completely, drowning us in shadows, the sedan passed the first buildings at the edge of the town. More roads followed, each of them seeming identical to me. Houses upon houses, with the odd smattering of businesses and bars, restaurants and rundown motels between them. A monolithic high school interrupted the endless neighborhoods at one point, its old brick construction towering over the homes facing it from the other side of the street, and every few blocks seemed to reveal another church.

At a road like any other, Chloe's dad turned the sedan. He continued on for a few moments, and then he thumbed a button on a small box clipped to a visor above his head.

On a two-story, pale brown house with white shutters and a covered porch, the garage door began to roll upward. A yellowed light bulb came on when the door finished opening, illuminating the random assortment of tools, cleaning supplies and metal shelves inside. Flicking the turn signal briefly, he guided the sedan from the road into the driveway and then pulled into the garage. He tapped the tiny box again, leaving the door to roll down behind us, and then turned off the engine. Wordlessly, Linda pushed open her door and left the car.

I looked to Chloe while her father got out as well.

She didn't move.

"Hey," I said quietly.

She swallowed hard and gave a quick nod. Not looking at me, she shoved open the door and then climbed from the car.

I eyed her curiously, uncertain what that had been about.

Still waiting for the tension to break and something to finally explode, I trailed Chloe and her family into their house.

6

CHLOE

The steps from the garage clunked under my feet. I followed Dad through the door and past the laundry room into the kitchen.

And I wondered if I had made a mistake.

They weren't speaking to me, but I knew that would change. The moment we were alone, everything would pick up where it left off – though, really, silence was almost as bad as yelling in its own special, drawn-out-torment sort of way.

I should have kept running with Zeke. Maybe gone to Canada or something. Surely it was nice this time of year.

The smell of the house surrounded me, all cinnamon and clove and alien after my weeks away. With his good arm – the one that wasn't in that horrible white sling – Dad reached over to flip on the light switch. As the fixture overhead flickered to life, he continued through the kitchen toward the living room.

I paused. On the breakfast table below the back window, I

could see abandoned dishes. Beside the refrigerator, a gallon of milk still sat on the green laminate counter. A striped dish towel lay in a rumpled heap on the tile floor as well, the whole mess so unlike my parents that it was startling.

They'd left in a rush. They'd been worried.

My throat tightened. I hurried through the room, leaving Zeke to follow me.

By the fireplace, Mom was murmuring something heated to Dad.

She cut off the moment I appeared at the doorway.

Dad put a hand to hers as though trying to calm her. "Would you ask your friend to wait in the kitchen, Chloe?"

I could hear the careful choice of words. Cautiously, I glanced to Zeke.

He nodded. Taking my hand and giving it a brief squeeze, he eyed my parents for a heartbeat and then headed for the breakfast table.

My feet sank into the brown shag carpet as I walked into the living room. Mom and Dad took a seat on the overstuffed couch beneath their pictures of the Gobi Desert and Death Valley, leaving the armchair across from them to me.

It felt familiar. So many of our arguments had started this way.

Though they usually ended with slammed doors and more silence.

I glanced over, grateful that I could see Zeke through the archway connecting us to the kitchen.

"What happened, Chloe?" Dad asked.

Blinking, I looked back at him.

His gaze twitched to my neck.

I shook my head. "Nothing. A guy... we handled it. It's fine."

They stared at me.

"Someone tried to *kill* you," Mom demanded. "And you 'handled it'?"

I paused. I did not want to get into this. Desperately.

"Yeah."

She exhaled, looking away as though she couldn't believe anything about me or what I'd just said.

"And will this guy be looking for you?" Dad asked.

I swallowed. "I don't think so. Not... not here."

He paused. "By the ocean then."

I gave a tiny shrug.

"How did you make it to Nebraska?"

I tried not to fidget on the chair, feeling like I was in an interrogation. My gaze flicked to Zeke. "We stole the guy's truck."

Mom made an incredulous noise, the sound so familiar I could feel my blood start boiling. My nails dug into my palms with the effort of not letting anger get the better of me.

"It ran out of gas, so we called you," I finished.

Dad's mouth thinned. "So this wasn't a dehaian?"

"No."

He glanced to Mom, who was staring at the brown chenille

of the couch and shaking her head.

I looked between them. "What?"

"Are you in pain? From the... the ocean?" Dad asked.

"No."

Mom turned back sharply. "Then you'll stay," she said, a weird mix of insistence and hope in her tone.

I hesitated. "For now."

She exhaled again. It almost seemed like she was fighting back tears. My brow flickered down.

"We would like it very much if you would," Dad said to me carefully.

I didn't know how to respond. But for a few moments here and there, they weren't acting *remotely* like themselves. Like the erratic, no-explanation, dictatorial crazies I'd grown up with. It was like they were scared of something. A real something, not just the made-up stuff they'd always pretended to fear.

And as impossible as it seemed, it kind of felt like it was me.

"O-okay," I managed.

"Thank you," he said.

My brow furrowed incredulously.

"But," he continued, "while you *are* here... we'd like to ask you not to discuss your trip with anyone. Just to be on the safe side."

My confusion deepened. "What? Why?"

"There are a couple other landwalkers in town. We'd prefer

if you avoided speaking with them about your trip."

I stared at him. "A couple other... who?"

He looked to Mom again. "Chief Reynolds and his nephew, Aaron Erlich."

I blinked at the names of two of the local police officers.

"Everyone is already aware you ran away to California. There's no fixing that. After the events in that ambulance, the Delaneys told the police you had been kidnapped before we could ask them to create another story."

I blinked again. Peter and Diane had reported me *kidnapped*?

"But we'd appreciate it if you didn't volunteer any information about that. We'll need to come up with an explanation for your return, and your bruises as well, but barring that story to the police, please remain silent on the entire subject."

I heard the words, filing them away somewhere in my head while I tried to sort out the rest. Police. We were going to have to talk to the police. Because they thought I'd been kidnapped.

My stomach rolled.

I guess I couldn't blame the Delaneys for their story. Marty and Colin had stolen me and Baylie away from the cabin, something that had been witnessed by the other EMTs at the scene, and then I'd vanished into the ocean. There probably hadn't been much the Delaneys *could* say.

But still... *kidnapped*. And from an ambulance where two men died.

Where I'd killed one of them.

The nausea grew worse. True, that'd been self-defense and halfway an accident as well, but I couldn't explain that to anyone. Colin had been trying to inject me with a drug that could have killed me if Noah hadn't gotten me to the ocean in time. I'd just been trying to stop him. But the spikes from my arms had left a straight, savagely deep row of stab wounds in Colin's chest.

I doubted anyone had come up with an explanation for those.

And now I'd have to create one for the police.

The *landwalker* police…

I let out a breath. It was hard to know what to think. Chief Reynolds was like a cartoon, all gregarious and rotund and white-haired like Santa Claus in a brown police uniform. I was fairly certain he knew each person in Reidsburg by name, and could probably quote their life history as well. His nephew was his scrawny opposite, though: a shy guy with big glasses who looked like he belonged buried in a chemistry lab someplace. Only two years ahead of me in school, Aaron had been raised by his uncle and he'd taken up with the police force at his first opportunity, something that I supposed should have garnered respect. But with a build like a scarecrow and an awkwardness that meant he could barely answer a direct question, no one in Reidsburg had ever seen him as anything but a product of nepotism or a joke.

Except my parents, anyway. They'd just gone out of their

way to avoid him and his uncle alike.

And suddenly, that didn't seem like simply another symptom of their insanity. Not entirely.

"Are they dangerous?" I asked.

Dad glanced to Mom. "They think you're our daughter," he allowed awkwardly. "Biological daughter, I mean."

I swallowed. There was that. And I didn't want to get into that.

"How do you know they're... like you?" I asked instead.

"We checked with the elders."

My brow knitted again. "The who?"

Dad paused. "The elders. They're... well, they're rather like leaders among the landwalkers. We don't have any way of just *knowing* who is one of us and who's simply human. The line is blurry anyway. There aren't many of what you'd call 'purebloods' left. None, actually. We've been among humans for so long, we've all got them in our ancestry. In fact, there comes a point where some folks... well, they're so much more human than landwalker, there's nothing really *landwalker* in them. Just odd traits like a tendency toward bad seasickness, or a fear of the ocean and the creatures in it. And otherwise, they're human.

"But if we *do* want to know about others like us, there are the elders. They're not old, necessarily; some are younger than your mother and me. But they're men and women who," he glanced to Mom, "perhaps are more in touch with what we used to be, I guess you could say. And a long time back, maybe a few centuries or more, they started keeping track of our people. Making genealogies, as well as maintaining stories from our history so that as a culture, we wouldn't just be completely absorbed into the humans. They're the ones who let us know about other landwalkers in our area."

Warily, I watched them. "And it'd be dangerous if they knew about me? About…"

I trailed off, not sure if I should bring up the fact I was adopted. My mom – my biological mom, or real mom, or something – was Dad's sister, Susan. My actual, real, or whatever dad was a dehaian named Kreyus, whom no one had ever heard from again. And until a Sylphaen had nearly killed me in Santa Lucina a few weeks before, Bill and Linda Kowalski had never told me about either of them.

Instead, they'd lied to me. They'd let me believe I was their daughter by birth. They'd never mentioned a word about the dehaians, the landwalkers, or how turning into the former could kill me because I was half of the latter.

And short of screaming at them – *again* – I still wasn't sure how to talk about that.

Dad hesitated. "Half-dehaian, half-landwalker kids… like we told you. They don't usually survive. The ones who do grow up a bit…" He glanced to Mom again. "We've heard stories. Some landwalker folks who are enamored of the idea that they could change our situation. Become dehaian again and all that. So they take these kids who manage to survive infancy, and they push them. See if they can learn anything about integrating dehaian traits back into us. But that just speeds up the destabilizing of the two sides of those kids' heritage. The dehaian side is stronger. It overwhelms them, and then they die."

I shivered.

"We don't know for certain if it's true," Dad continued carefully, "but honey, that's part of why we kept everything a secret. Let Chief Reynolds and his nephew just think you were our..." A pained expression flickered across his face. "Our girl."

I couldn't breathe.

"We didn't want to risk that someone might hear about you, and might try to steal you away from us to do that to you. And now that you're... well..."

"Alive?" I offered, my voice choked.

"Please just don't tell anyone about this," he finished.

I looked over to find Zeke watching me. His brow twitched up, every line of his face and body making clear how he'd come into the living room in a heartbeat if I just gave him a sign.

My gaze dropped to the carpet.

"It would also be better," Mom added, her voice cautious like she was afraid something might break. "If your friend went back to his home."

"What? No."

The response came out fast, and harsh too, and my gaze snapped up from the ground to glare at her.

Her face tightened, as though arguing with me and trying to tell me what to do had suddenly become difficult for her. "Chloe, I... Whatever you think you're feeling toward him, you can't... it's not..."

I stared at her in confusion as she struggled for words.

"He's dangerous," she concluded. "He's dehaian, and if anyone finds out he's–"

"*I'm* dehaian."

"No, you're our Chloe," she countered fervently. "You are *not*–"

She cut off and turned away as Dad put a hand to her knee.

"Not what?" I demanded. "A fish? Scale-skin? Scum-sucker? What were you going to call us?"

Breathing hard, I stared at them.

"Like them," Mom whispered.

Still shaking with fury, I took a moment to respond. "And what does that mean?"

Dad gave a small glance to the kitchen. "I'd rather we not discuss this with–"

"*Say* it."

He paused, watching me. "Soulless."

My brow flickered down incredulously.

"The dehaians," he said, "when our people split from theirs, we each got a bit of what made us who we used to be. For them, it was the ability to live underwater. To change like they do. For us, we have the ability to live on land without pain, and apparently, well..."

He sighed. "I guess you'd call it humanity. The capacity to care about others. Dehaians... they're not like people, Chloe. Every story we've heard of them makes it clear they don't have feelings like us, and that they use the feelings of others for their entertainment. They enjoy manipulating people and their emotions, and they don't care about the consequences or the suffering. They even use magic to force people to become obsessed with them, just so they can watch–"

"Wait, *that*?"

"They kill people with 'that', honey. For fun."

I stared at him. "No, they–"

"That's not true."

Zeke's voice made me stop, and I looked over to see him standing by the archway, his gaze on my parents.

"Only sick freaks do that. And it's illegal. Using it at *all* on non-dehaians is illegal, and what you're describing, we view as murder."

I turned back to Mom and Dad.

Dad's mouth compressed briefly. "Chloe, of course he'd say that. They're manipulators, only interested in getting what they want. But if you understood what they are truly capable–"

"I *do* understand," I interrupted.

"Then you'd understand that this boy has probably used it on you!" Mom cried. "Everything you're arguing for him could just be a result of what he's done!"

"It doesn't work that way."

"Chloe, they–"

91

"It doesn't! Not between dehaians. For us, it–" I cut off, discomfort catching up with me, and I fought to keep myself from blushing. "It's not like that."

She shook her head. "You can't be sure, Chloe. Please. You're *not* one of them; you're like us. You wouldn't know what it is or if he–"

"I've used it," I said.

She froze, her face a picture of shock and horror.

"We both have," I continued. "The man who attacked us, when he was strangling me, I used it to stop him. And Zeke helped a friend–"

"Your daughter," he interrupted.

I turned to him in confused surprise. In the cave, he'd told me he'd been trying to keep someone from dying.

He hadn't mentioned anything about it being me.

Zeke didn't take his eyes from my parents. "When she was in the hospital and the damage that Sylphaen bastard had done was killing her, I had medicine from back home that could help. But I needed to get past emergency room security, so I used that ability you're describing. Aveluria. Just a bit, so the woman recovered. And your daughter did too."

He paused, and when he spoke again, his voice shook with quiet intensity. "We care."

They stared at him.

"Zeke's saved my life over the past few weeks, Mom. He's done it more times than I can count, even when it meant he might die." I trembled. "Dehaians aren't monsters, no matter

92

what those stories say."

She blinked as she dropped her gaze from his. "It's still not safe," she persisted. "He shouldn't even be able to *be* here—"

"Everything we know says your kind can't go much more than a hundred miles from a coast," Dad said to Zeke, a note of challenge in his voice. "And yet here you are."

Zeke glanced to me, not answering.

"I did that," I supplied quietly.

Mom's brow furrowed.

"I don't know how," I continued before they could ask. "I just know that it's working."

She glanced to Dad, obviously seeking help. "T-that may be, but he still needs to leave. If he becomes sick at the wrong moment..."

"If he goes, I go."

She looked back at me in alarm. "Chloe, you—"

"I mean it."

My heart raced as Mom stared at me, her brow twitching down. I'd never gotten away with demands like this. Ever. But they weren't acting like themselves, and this was important. I didn't know, if he left, how far Zeke could travel before the pull of the ocean came back.

And killed him.

With effort, Mom tugged her gaze to Dad. "Bill?" she tried.

Dad drew a slow breath. "Alright. Fine. The boy will stay... for now."

Without another word, he pushed to his feet and headed

for the hall. Mom rose from the couch as well, hesitancy written all over her.

"Well, um… in that case… are you hungry?" she asked. "I could cook something?"

I stared at her, so taken back by her uncharacteristic behavior, I didn't quite know what to do.

"Uh, sure," I answered, knowing we'd both eaten only a few hours before and could probably keep going for a day or two if necessary. But I couldn't tell her that. She almost seemed desperate. "Food would be nice."

She nodded. Clutching her hands together, she started for the kitchen, only to balk at Zeke still standing in the archway.

He stepped aside. She skirted past him.

His brow rose as he glanced back at me.

I shook my head in bafflement. Getting up from the chair, I walked over to him. He took my hand and I drew a breath, feeling a bit of my tension leak out just at having him there.

"Chloe," Dad called.

I tensed all over again. I looked down the hall to find him at the base of the stairs.

"You should probably get cleaned up before dinner."

I hesitated, reading the stern way he was watching us.

Zeke squeezed my hand. I glanced back.

"Be right here," he whispered.

My lip twitched up in a grateful smile.

"Chloe," Dad said again, his voice even harder.

"Coming," I replied.

Squeezing Zeke's hand as well, I nodded and then headed for the stairs.

The steps creaked under me and when I reached the second floor, everything was still. Not bothering to look back to where I knew Dad watched me at the base of the stairs, I continued down the brown-carpeted hallway, only to pause when I came to the white wood of my bedroom door.

My hand rose and the door swung aside at my touch. Reaching past the doorframe, I flipped on the light.

Sterile white walls with pictures of the Sahara met my gaze. The brown quilt with its crosshatched patterns of wheat covered my twin bed against the far wall. A few snapshots of me and Baylie stood on the oak dresser, trapped in bronze frames. On the window, the heavy, tan curtains were closed, sealing out the darkness.

I barely felt like I recognized it all. Only a few weeks had passed, but in that time I'd lived under the ocean. I'd swum with royalty through a palace the size of a mountain and fled from mercenaries God-knew-how-far beneath the sea.

And now...

A shaky breath left me. I stepped into the room, feeling like I was walking into another reality. The backpack I'd taken to California was tucked against the side of my bed, and my cell phone and wallet were on the nightstand nearby.

I glanced to the window and the closed curtains. Baylie could be home. The lights at her house had been off when we drove up, and most of the curtains had been closed, but she still could be. After all, our stay at the Delaneys was supposed to have ended over a week ago.

But then, she'd still been in Santa Lucina when I called the day before Zeke and I left.

I swallowed. Maybe she was here. Or maybe Peter and Diane had shipped it or something.

Mom cleared her throat behind me and I jumped.

"Would you like help?" she asked.

I stared, confused. That weird, worried look was on her face again. "Help?"

"Putting your stuff away," she elaborated.

My expression didn't change. "That's alright."

She hesitated, seeming as though she still wanted to try. She gave me a jerky nod and didn't leave.

The silence stretched.

"So I wondered what you might like for dinner?" Mom asked. "I thought maybe we could see if anywhere in town carries sushi."

I made myself blink. *Sushi?* She–

"If you'd like," Mom pressed on hastily. "I just… I want you to feel… what I mean is, I heard that's similar to what they eat, and if you need to have food like they do, then we can find it."

I shook my head. "Whatever you make is fine for both of

us," I managed. I paused. "Mom, what is this?"

"Nothing," she replied, a touch of familiar defensiveness coming into her voice. "You're my daughter. I'm not going to starve you."

I looked away.

"I'm sorry," she said.

My eyebrows rose as I turned back in surprise at the words.

"I'll make barbecue chicken," she continued. "Your favorite. Is that good?"

"Y-yeah. Thanks."

Giving me a tense smile, she moved to leave and then hesitated, looking back. "I want you to know," she said tightly, "we're happy you came home. I know things are... are tense sometimes. But we're really just..."

Mom's brow furrowed and, as impossible as it seemed, she actually looked like she was trying not to cry.

Swallowing hard, she forced her expression to clear. "We always want what's best for you, Chloe. That's all. And so if there's anything you need in order for you to be okay here, you just let me know. Anything in the world, understand?"

I stared and succeeded in moving my head in something like a nod.

Mom echoed the motion. Without another word, she left the room.

It took me a moment to drag my gaze from the doorway, and a moment more before my thoughts ordered themselves enough to process what had just happened.

My mother… wanted to make things *okay* for me.

Okay for me.

A breath escaped me, the sound loud in the quiet.

My mother wanted to make things okay for me here.

I didn't know what to do. I'd thought coming home would be normal. I'd known what 'normal' meant – fights, months of being grounded, and my parents possibly even trying to move us out of town simply because I'd run off to California with Baylie – but after the past few weeks, I'd been willing to risk it.

But this…

This was a parallel dimension.

This was crazier than what I'd left. This was Mom and Dad acting in a way I'd never seen in my life.

Acting like they'd been scared I wouldn't come back.

I trembled at the memory of Zeke's words. I didn't know what I'd planned. I hadn't thought that far ahead. I'd just been trying to survive.

And now I'd returned to something as strange as anything I'd seen in the past few weeks.

Turning away from the door, I hurried toward my closet to get changed out of the clothes I'd worn for the past few days. I didn't want to be in here, in this familiar-alien room with the desert décor my parents had mandated all these years. I didn't know *how* to be here.

And Zeke was downstairs.

He was the only part of this new life of mine that still felt sane.

$\backsim 7 \backsim$

ZEKE

It'd been several hours since we'd arrived at Chloe's parents' home.

The time had been awkward enough for several years.

On the makeshift bed Chloe's parents had put together on the couch, I lay with my arms behind my head, watching nothing in particular. The house was dark, everyone else having gone to bed a few hours before. Moonlight slipped through a gap between the curtains above me, turning a tiny measure of the night to paler shadows but otherwise leaving the blackness unchanged.

Dinner had been a silent affair but for small comments about passing various dishes. Her parents had hardly taken their eyes from us the whole time, and soon after the meal was finished, they'd herded Chloe back up to her bedroom again, from which I hadn't seen her since.

They were still scared of me, it was obvious. And still partly convinced I'd put some spell on their daughter, forcing her to be attracted to me. They didn't want us near each other, and had set up the table to keep us from sitting anywhere close. Truthfully, I was mildly surprised her father hadn't tried to bundle me out of the house the moment Chloe's back was turned.

Though, of course, there was always tomorrow.

I stared up at the sliver of moonlight. I hadn't let my eyes change to break the darkness, if only to keep her parents from freaking out if they came downstairs. They didn't seem to know much about dehaians, and the sight of my glowing eyes would probably only serve to make them think me more of a monster.

A sigh escaped me. As infuriating as it felt, in all honesty the ignorance was mutual. My whole life, I'd never heard of landwalkers. Or greliarans, for that matter. But then, my education had never touched on anything mythological. Dad hired tutors to teach us about politics and what we'd need to run the nation of Yvaria, not what I suspected he viewed as children's tales. The few times my grandfather, Jirral, had even *tried* telling us stories outside the 'real' world, Dad had stopped him, insisting that we only fill our heads with what was necessary for leadership of our people and survival.

A fact which would seem ironic, if it wasn't so painful.

I glanced to the kitchen as a small noise from the refrigerator broke the quiet. Tired as I was, I couldn't sleep. Everything felt too strange. I'd never stayed in a house at night before. I'd scarcely even been inside one. Dehaians didn't really like to go where we couldn't smell the sea air, reminding us as it did of the possibility of being trapped away from the ocean.

And now here I was, well over a thousand miles from the water.

I shifted on the flannel sheets, pushing the thought aside. I didn't know what would trigger the pain of the ocean's distance returning, or even if anything would at all, but I didn't want to risk it.

The memory was bad enough.

A creak came from the stairs. I glanced over.

Footsteps crept down the hall.

"Zeke?" Chloe whispered.

I sat up, the darkness vanishing as my eyes changed.

Chloe stood at the entrance to the living room in a t-shirt and cotton shorts much like she'd worn that first night I'd spoken to her on the beach. A relieved expression flashed across her face at the sight of my eyes, and her own took on an emerald glow as she crossed to the couch.

"You okay?" I asked as she sat down.

Chloe nodded. "Just... couldn't sleep."

I waited. Something in her voice made it seem like more than just nightmares keeping her awake.

She glanced to me. "You doing alright?"

"Yeah, I think so."

She nodded again, dropping her gaze to her folded hands.

A heartbeat passed.

"It's so weird being back," she said quietly. "I thought

after all the craziness of the past few weeks, it'd be normal somehow, but instead it's like... like the world turned at this funny angle when I wasn't looking and now I can't fit inside it anymore."

I hesitated, not sure what to say.

She caught sight of my expression and shook her head. "I don't know," she sighed.

I put my arm around her. A tiny smile pulled at her lip as she leaned her head against my shoulder.

"You mind if I stay down here with you?" she asked.

I chuckled. "Mind?"

Her smile grew.

I shifted around, lying back on the couch again. She curled up beside me, her cheek on my chest and her leg resting on mine.

A breath left her as I wrapped my arms around her. Straying up my skin, her fingers brushed my neck before settling on my chest as well.

"I'm going to miss you when you go," she whispered.

My arms tightened on her, holding her close. "I don't want to think about that yet."

She nodded.

Silence fell back on the room, but for the hum of the refrigerator and the soft noises from bugs outside. My eyes drifted shut as I breathed in deep the smell of her hair, which still carried hints of salt and the sea.

I felt her move away and I opened my eyes.

Surprise hit me. It was morning.

"Shh," Chloe whispered to me.

And then she fled across the room to the kitchen.

I didn't have long to be confused.

Bill came around the base of the stairs. Wearing flannel pants and a cotton t-shirt, he looked like he'd just woken. He paused at the sight of me, a wary sort of suspicion in his eyes, and then continued into the living room. His gaze swept the space, finding Chloe.

Keeping her back to him, she was busy with taking a bowl from the cabinet. A box of something sat on the counter next to her, and as I watched, she reached over and then poured the contents into the bowl.

He headed into the kitchen. Snagging my shirt from the arm of the couch, I put it on quickly and then rose to my feet, watching him.

"Go get dressed," I heard him tell her, his displeasure clear and his voice brooking no argument.

She hesitated and then gave a quick nod. Without a word, she retreated from the kitchen and moved fast for the stairs, her gaze flashing to me as she passed.

I could see the worry in her eyes.

As she disappeared around the landing, I looked back at her father.

Standing by the archway to the kitchen, he regarded me, his dislike for me obvious.

And a good amount of his anger too.

"Was Chloe down here with you last night?" he demanded.

I paused. The truth might get me kicked out. But from his expression, I seriously doubted he'd believe me if I lied.

"She had trouble sleeping," I answered. "We didn't do anything."

The anger strengthened. "I don't want you touching her, understand?"

"I understand."

His face tightened at my response. I could tell he didn't believe me.

Which was fair. I understood he didn't want me around his daughter.

It just meant little to me compared to what Chloe might want.

"You listen close," he growled, stalking toward me. "You're here on my sufferance, do you get me? And the moment Chloe calms down after all she's been through, you're going home. Now I'll admit all those stories we've heard may not be true. But I'm willing to bet some are. Like the one that ended Chloe's mom up pregnant with her when she was scarcely more than Chloe's age, and then dead not long after."

I tensed. There was a possibility between those lines – one that would explain his hatred for us – and nausea twisted my stomach at the thought of it.

The pull of aveluria magic would have been brutal on a landwalker.

"My girl is still a kid," Bill continued. "She may not think so, and maybe neither do you, but it's the truth. She's got her whole life ahead of her, and she doesn't need trouble coming down on her because of the likes of you. So you keep your hands off her, do I make myself clear?"

I paused. Defending myself wouldn't do any good. Especially since, when it came to me and Chloe, the moment she was ready for things between us to go farther, I'd sooner move to the depths of the desert than deny her.

And his daughter wasn't a landwalker. Whether he accepted that or not, I still couldn't hurt her the way Chloe's biological father might have hurt her mom.

"Yes," I replied.

Footsteps thudded on the steps as Chloe jogged back to the first floor.

Bill cast a quick look to the stairway. "Good," he said to me.

Without another word, he returned to the kitchen, keeping an eye toward me while he went.

Chloe whipped around the turn of the landing and headed down the hall. A dark brown t-shirt had replaced her pajamas, along with a pair of jean shorts that fit her so well, it took a fair amount of effort for me not to show any expression at the sight of her in them. Around her neck, she'd wrapped a thick and glittering green scarf that set off her eyes and covered her bruises at the same time. As she reached the living room entryway, she paused, and her gaze twitched between me and her father. "Everything okay?" she mouthed to me.

SKYE MALONE

I didn't respond, returning my attention to him.

It felt rather like having a shark in the room. One I couldn't attack.

Glancing between me and her dad again, she started across the room toward me.

I shook my head. She stopped, her brow twitching down warily.

Linda came down the stairs. As she spotted me, I saw the same look flash through her eyes as she'd had yesterday. The one that said she suspected me of magically brainwashing her daughter.

It was hard to keep the frustration from my face.

Wringing her hands, Linda walked to the entrance to the living room, her gaze darting between us as though she was afraid Chloe would evaporate or I'd suddenly decide to stab someone through the heart.

"Are you..." Linda started to her. "Are you feeling okay this morning?"

"Fine," Chloe replied. She inched farther into the living room, leaving her mother by the doorway. "Um, listen. Is Baylie home? I saw my stuff from California upstairs last night and then just now I thought I spotted her through the window."

Linda looked to her husband.

"Have you spoken to Baylie about any of this?" Bill asked.

Chloe tensed. "No."

He exhaled.

"I need to talk to her, though," she continued, obviously seeing his reluctance. "She hasn't seen me since the Sylphaen attacked the cabin. She's got to be worried."

His mouth tightened.

"Or are you still going to insist we move away and I never speak to her again because she helped me get to California?" she finished, anger threading through her tone.

Bill's face darkened. "We are trying to protect you, Chloe. If she doesn't know about this, there's no reason for you to talk to her now."

"But what about that kidnapping you said the Delaneys reported to the cops? She might think I–"

"No."

She stared at him.

"If Chloe saw Baylie through the window," I pointed out, "how do you know Baylie didn't see her?"

Her father's gaze snapped to me, his fury at my comment clear.

"Yeah," Chloe agreed, a touch desperately. "What if she did? She could be calling the police right now. And she'll definitely see me sooner or later. What are you going to do then?"

"Fine," Linda said. "Then we will go speak to her on your behalf–"

"You're not doing that!"

"Chloe–"

"No!" She looked between her parents. "If Baylie's there, then I'm going to see her. And I *am* going to talk to her. End of discussion."

She moved toward me.

"Okay," her father agreed.

She stopped, eyeing him warily.

"Okay," Bill repeated. "You go talk to her. But you will tell her only what we give you to say. You don't remember your attacker, or anything of what happened. You woke in a barn and ran till you found a gas station payphone and called us. You've been here for a week and you haven't wanted to talk to anyone. That's it. No other explanation; nothing of dehaians, landwalkers or anything."

His gaze twitched to me. I tensed. "And that boy stays here."

"I'm not—"

"Or he's out the door right now."

A breath escaped her.

"Please understand, Chloe," Linda pled. "We're not trying to be unreasonable; we just want you to be safe. This is for your own good."

Chloe glanced at her, incredulity in her eyes.

"What will it be?" Bill asked.

I could see Chloe trembling. "Alright," she answered, her voice tight. "But Zeke comes with me. I'm not leaving him here so you can kick him out while I'm gone."

Bill tensed.

She gave him a dark look. "I'm not that stupid, Dad."

"And how do you propose to explain him to her?" he asked.

Chloe was silent.

Bill watched her for a heartbeat. "Tell her he's your cousin. He came when he heard you were missing."

"Baylie knows I don't have any cousins."

"Tell her you lied."

Chloe stared at him.

"Tell her you lied," Bill repeated firmly. "Say you don't like others to know about him."

"But–"

"Chloe."

Still shaking, she hesitated, and then gave a tight nod. "Fine."

She took my hand.

And she didn't let go till we reached the door.

At a fast pace, she descended the porch stairs, and when she reached the yard, she strode toward the green, two-story house next door in a way that made me think she was barely restraining herself from running. We crossed the concrete driveway and hurried past the tall wooden fence that surrounded the next backyard. Still shaking with fury, Chloe marched up the steps to the porch and the white front door.

And then she paused. Uncertainty seemed to filter past the rage on her face and, breathing hard, she glanced to me.

I tried for a reassuring smile.

Her lip twitched gratefully.

Exhaling quickly, Chloe reached up and knocked on the door.

8

CHLOE

The waiting was the worst.

Standing by the door, I resisted the urge to knock again.

Or run away.

Because, really, I had no idea what I was going to tell Baylie. I wouldn't lie. I didn't care what my parents wanted. I wasn't going to lie to my best friend.

But I didn't know how to explain either.

My hand quivered. She was here. I couldn't see her car in the driveway, but she and her parents usually parked in their garage anyway. I'd spotted her through the window, though. Just for a second, blurry and vaguely shadowed by the distance, but I had.

Growing up next to each other for thirteen years, I'd know her silhouette anywhere.

Footsteps thudded on the stairs inside.

I fought the impulse to turn and run.

Baylie tugged open the door and then froze.

I swallowed. "Hey."

She gaped at me, blinked, and then suddenly leaned past the doorframe and threw a quick look around the neighborhood.

"Uh, hey," she said, sounding choked. "C-come in."

She retreated from the doorway, leaving us space to join her in the front room. Her gaze flicked over me and Zeke, and I could see the questions in her eyes.

And the nervousness.

My brow furrowed while we came inside. The house seemed normal. A television was playing upstairs, a trio of library books were stacked on the corner table, and Baylie's backpack sat by the door. Nothing else had changed. Yet Baylie seemed like she was hurrying us into the fort before the bloodthirsty hordes attacked.

And she had vivid bruises on her arms.

I stared, the rest of the room forgotten. Her palms were bandaged, while purplish-blue marks ringed her forearms, each bruise several inches across.

My heart started to pound. Noah wouldn't have hurt her. I'd gambled on that. Bet that he'd never touch his stepsister, even when he'd been such a monster to me.

And yet...

"What happened to your arms?" I asked.

She didn't answer. Swiftly, she scanned the neighborhood again and then shut the door.

And locked it.

"Baylie?" I pressed.

She turned away from the door, crossed the three steps between us, and threw her arms around me.

"Oh God, I'm so glad you're okay," she breathed as she squeezed me. "When did you get here?"

I hugged her back, giving Zeke an incredulous look while I did. "Last night. Baylie, what's going on?"

She exhaled, hanging onto me a moment longer, and then she let go. In the den, the back door slid shut. Baylie cast a quick glance toward the sound. "It's a long story." She tugged at one of her bandages. "We, um–"

Footsteps interrupted her. His attention on the phone in his hand, Noah strode into the room from the hall. "Baylie, that was Maddox. He can't get here till Thursday, so I'm going to head back–"

He glanced up. His feet came to a stop.

"Chloe," he said.

I felt paralyzed. I stared at him, my mind trying to catch up with the reality of him standing there in the archway to the hall, his green eyes shocked and the phone in his hand forgotten, when all I could see was his face, cracked with light and furious as he hurled insults and threatened to kill me if I didn't leave the beach.

Air forced its way into my lungs. I retreated a step to Zeke's side, barely keeping spikes from coming out on my arms. "Noah. W-what are you…"

He seemed to have trouble breathing too. Blinking, he

tugged his gaze from me. "I, um–"

His attention caught on Zeke and he cut off, his brow furrowing in sudden confusion.

"I invited Noah to come back with me," Baylie supplied warily, watching us all.

Zeke put a hand to my back. "Let's go," he said darkly.

Noah tensed, his gaze flicking toward where Zeke touched me and then returning to my face.

"Wait, why?" Baylie asked. She looked between us. "Chloe, you can't. There's–"

"It wasn't what you thought," Noah interjected, watching me.

My brow twitched down.

"I had to do that," he continued. "I... my cousins were at the house. They're like me, except... except they want to hurt you. I had to get you out of there. Make sure you didn't come back so you'd be safe from them."

He paused. "I'm sorry. Everything I said... I swear I didn't mean any of it."

I stared at him. I couldn't find words. They just weren't there. And I didn't know what they'd be anyway.

He'd been horrible. Terrifying. I'd never seen...

Noah took a step toward me. "Chloe, I–"

Moving fast, Zeke pushed me behind him, never taking his eyes from Noah.

Noah stopped, his focus snapping from me to Zeke. Baylie stared at us, obviously baffled.

"Wait," I managed. I put my hand to Zeke's arm. His head turned toward me, though he didn't look away from Noah. "What... *what* happened?"

"How is he here?" Noah asked instead.

I struggled to come up with a response when all I wanted was for him to explain again. His cousins. He had cousins?

"Chloe?" Noah pressed.

"She doesn't owe you any–" Zeke started.

"Me." My voice was tight. "I, um..."

I couldn't finish. Noah's brow furrowed.

"Guys?" Baylie tried with a nervous glance to the front of the house. "You think we could move away from the windows?"

More confusion rose in me, but Noah's face just tightened.

"Yeah," he said. Still watching me and Zeke, he nodded toward the hall and then headed that way.

Zeke glanced to me.

I hesitated and then followed Noah to the den. Two steps led us down to the familiar, cream-carpeted space where Baylie and I had spent countless evenings watching movies, talking about school, and generally avoiding my parents. A fireplace filled the leftmost wall, while a large television occupied another corner and an aging couch that I knew for a fact was the most comfortable thing on the planet sat below the back window. The room was long, taking up as it did the entire rear side of the house, and two more steps led up to a glass door that opened out onto the fenced backyard.

Noah stopped in the middle of the room and waited till

Baylie had pulled the accordion door to the hallway closed before speaking.

"So you…" He grimaced. "You're here. Are you okay?" he asked me. "It doesn't hurt?"

I shook my head.

He nodded as though reassured, but his expression was still tight when he glanced to Zeke.

"You think someone could tell me what's going on?" Baylie asked into the silence. "*Finally?*"

I hesitated. I didn't know what to say.

"Or perhaps why we're afraid of windows?" Zeke added darkly, watching Noah and the views of the backyard equally.

Noah paused. "My cousins are in town. They tracked you here."

A breath left me. "The ones who want to hurt me?"

"So you say," Zeke added.

I could see the rage in Noah's eyes.

"Hey!" Baylie snapped, coming to Noah's side and glaring at Zeke. "Who do you think you are, huh? Chloe, who is this guy?"

I didn't answer her. "You never mentioned cousins."

"I don't like to advertise," Noah retorted. "But yeah. Them. And my uncle. They came by yesterday and seemed to believe you'd be able to make it back here."

Suspicion stole over me. "What were they driving?"

His eyes narrowed. "Red SUV."

I swallowed. Zeke looked like he was barely restraining a

curse.

"And I suppose you're related to Earl too?" Zeke demanded.

"Earl?" Noah repeated, confused.

"Big guy," Zeke supplied. "Lives in the forest with his knives and a serious dead-daughter obsession."

Noah shook his head warily.

I hesitated. He didn't appear to be lying.

And I wished I could trust that. But he'd also attacked Zeke that day on the beach, and threatened to kill me as well. I couldn't shake the memory of the disgust in his eyes, no matter how much he claimed not to have meant it.

Carefully, I lifted a hand to my neck and pulled down the edge of the scarf.

He froze.

"We've run into…" I gave a tense glance to Baylie, "into a guy who wanted us dead before."

Noah stared at the bruises. He looked sick. Genuine, honest-to-God sick.

"Chloe…" Baylie breathed. "What the…"

"I-I don't know him," Noah managed. "I swear. The others… I don't have any connection to them."

I studied his face, seeing only nausea and concern, both of which were growing stronger by the second. Nothing remained of that hideous revulsion for me he'd shown on the beach. Nothing to say he was anything other than appalled at what Earl had done.

Trying to keep my hand from trembling, I tugged the scarf

back into place. "Why couldn't you just *tell* me?" I asked Noah, old hurt rising up inside. "On the beach, you could have—"

"I didn't have time. They... we can feel each other's presence. Know where others like us are, even if we can't see each other. And they were coming right behind me. As it was... Chloe, if you'd been a *second* slower in leaving..."

He exhaled, seeming to struggle for words. "They've spent their whole lives hoping to find someone like you. Just waiting for the chance to kill a... a person like you. I couldn't let them do that."

I shivered, remembering Earl's words about his daughter keeping his spirits up about finally finding us someday.

"Earl said something like that too," I allowed.

Noah managed a nod.

I glanced to Zeke.

"Why do they want to kill us?" he asked.

Noah hesitated, seeming like he'd rather not answer the question.

"Noah?" I pressed.

He exhaled. "We..." His jaw worked for a moment and his deep green gaze twitched to me. "We were created to kill you."

My brow drew down. "Created to...?"

"Long time ago. Old war. Bunch of..." Noah's gaze flicked to Baylie this time. He looked like the words were being dragged from him. "Bunch of old wizards. Dead island.

Dead civilization. Story is, they were being overrun and," he paused, "and they wanted a defense."

I stared at him. He'd told me greliaran meant 'protector' that day he'd driven me to the ocean after the Sylphaen had injected me.

He'd just never said protector against whom.

"Overrun?" I repeated.

He nodded.

I looked to Zeke. His brow shrugged slightly and he appeared as mystified as me.

"Overrun by what?" Baylie asked, her voice small.

I blinked. So tense I could see her shaking, she watched us with fear in her eyes.

Like we might be monsters. Like we might grow three heads or turn into snake-beasts or something.

I felt sick.

"So you... you're not actually..." she started, her face making clear what she was struggling to say. Not like her.

Not human.

"No," I answered softly.

Her brow furrowed.

"Chloe's not like me, though," Noah cut in. "What I told you was the truth. And she wasn't trying to keep anything a secret either. It just happened that way. She only found out about this after she got to Santa Lucina."

I hesitated, unprepared for his help.

Or for how much I appreciated it.

"But what…" Baylie tried.

"Dehaian," I said. "That's, um…"

"Like mermaids," Noah finished.

Baylie seemed to choke. "You're…?"

"Yeah," I said.

She gave a soft gasp. Running a hand through her blonde hair, she retreated from us. She scanned the floor as if searching for answers there, and then she looked back up, finding Noah.

For a moment she studied her stepbrother.

She exhaled. Her gaze went back to me.

"You're a *mermaid*," she stated.

I managed a shrug.

Another breath left her.

And degenerated into a chuckle at the end.

"You're a…" She gave another gasping chuckle. "And he's not human either, is he?"

She twitched her chin toward Zeke.

I shook my head cautiously, uncertain what to make of her reaction.

"He's like you?"

I nodded.

She echoed the motion, her gaze dropping back to the floor. "Wow."

I glanced to Noah. He was watching Baylie.

"So that's where you were," Baylie continued. "When you were gone this whole time. You were… I mean…"

I nodded again.

"Wow."

She paced away, running her fingers through her hair once more.

"How many others are there?" she asked, looking back at us. "I mean you're," she gestured to Noah, "what you are. Chloe and this guy are like mermaids... merpeople... what'd you call it again?"

"Dehaian," Zeke said.

Baylie eyed him distrustfully, but she jerked her head in cautious acknowledgement. "Dehaian. So who else? Who else isn't human around here?"

I hesitated, uncertain if we should go into this.

"Chloe?" she demanded.

"Um... Mom and Dad are landwalkers," I risked saying.

"And what the hell is that?"

"Like former dehaians. But they can't go near the water anymore."

Baylie nodded. "Great. Okay."

"You alright?" Noah asked.

She turned to him, incredulity in her blue eyes.

"Sorry," he amended.

She let out a breath. Blinking a few times, she shook her head and then looked at me again. "We need to talk."

I hesitated.

"But not now," she continued, coming back toward me. "Now..." She glanced to Noah. "Now there are five guys we've *really* got to get out of town."

He nodded.

"If they've been searching for dehaians their whole lives," I said, distantly feeling relief at being able to use the word with Baylie even in the midst of everything. "They're not going to leave easy."

"What if we—"

Zeke cut off as someone knocked on the front door.

"You expecting anyone?" he asked.

Baylie shook her head. She looked to Noah. "Is it them?"

He regarded the accordion door to the hall as though he could see through it to the outside. "Not unless they're hiding."

My brow started to draw down, and then I remembered what he'd said about knowing where others like him were.

The distant sound of the television cut off. Footsteps thudded on the stairs from the second floor, and then I heard the door open. Muffled voices followed, one of which sounded like Baylie's stepmom, Sandra.

"Just some guy," Noah supplied quietly, his eyes on the accordion door. "Says he's moving to the area with his daughter. He's asking about schools, neighbors."

He caught sight of me watching him, and a touch of embarrassment crossed his face. "We—"

"Have good hearing. Yeah, we know that part."

Noah hesitated and then gave a small nod, still seeming uncomfortable.

I pulled my gaze back to the others. "We could try to

make those guys think we've left. That maybe we *were* here, but now—"

A cry from the front of the house brought me up short. Footsteps pounded on the floor of the hallway.

Noah raced for the accordion door.

It ripped open before he got there.

Earl stopped, one massive hand holding chunks of the brown wood and the other gripping the doorframe. Breathing hard, he stood for a moment, his giant form filling the doorway and his eyes sweeping the room wildly.

His gaze landed on me. A wretched grin spasmed across his lip.

"Found you," he growled.

He charged at me, taking the two stairs to the den floor in a single step and throwing the remnants of the door to the ground as he came.

"Run!" Noah yelled at us, moving to block his path.

Earl barely paused. Fissures sped through his skin like an earthquake on overdrive, and in a heartbeat, fire lit his eyes. He swung an arm, batting Noah aside.

Zeke lunged at him, spikes on his arms.

With a snarl, Earl grabbed for him and Zeke ducked fast. His spikes slashed at the man's side, tearing through his flannel shirt, but the blades deflected uselessly from Earl's skin. Zeke spun, his arm arcing up, his spikes aimed at the man's face, but Earl twisted and snagged the blow in midair. With an angry shout, he hurled Zeke away as well.

Earl didn't stop.

I backpedaled, spikes rushing out of my forearms.

"You thought my friends wouldn't tell me where to look for you?" He scoffed. "You thought after what you did to me, I wouldn't hunt you down, you little scale-skinned *bitch?*"

The steps to the patio door bumped against my heels, and frantically, I fumbled behind me for the handle, my eyes locked on Earl.

Noah plowed into him. The television shattered as they crashed through it.

"Run, dammit!" Noah shouted, his greliaran form making the words a snarl.

Zeke rolled up from the ground and rushed at me. Grabbing my arm with one hand and yanking the door open with the other, he didn't spare Earl or Noah a glance.

"Baylie!" I yelled, stumbling after Zeke as he pulled me from the house.

A crash came from the den. White-faced, Baylie raced outside.

"Go!" she cried. "He's getting up!"

We ran for the back gate.

Glass shattered behind us. I couldn't tell what was happening in there. The gate latch broke at Zeke's tug at the flimsy padlock, and then we were out in the service way between the yards, barreling toward the street with Baylie fighting to keep up behind us.

I tried to slow. I'd forgotten how fast we were. Or, given

what Zeke had just done, how strong.

"We need to get out of sight," Zeke called as we bolted across the road.

I glanced to Baylie.

"Jefferson," she suggested breathlessly.

I nodded. Without another word, we both turned, running for the gap between two yards that we knew led to our school. Casting a look over his shoulder for Earl, Zeke followed.

The grassy expanse of the football practice field waited on the other side of the houses, with the block of bricks that was Thomas Jefferson High School beyond it. Football players getting in an early workout looked up and stared at us in confusion when we sped by.

"Where's the fire?" one yelled.

I ignored him and Baylie did too as we raced for the building's side. Left unlocked for the summer school students, the metal door surrendered to my yank on the handle and then clanged loudly when it slammed back against the brick wall. Our footsteps echoed as we ran through the hallways.

"Here," Baylie called.

We ducked into one of the empty classrooms. Tugging the door closed behind us, Zeke glanced around quickly and then strode past the desks to the strip of narrow windows along the opposite wall.

"Are you okay?" I asked him, casting a quick look to the hallway through the tiny square of glass in the door.

"Yeah," he replied as he yanked the vinyl curtains down.

I hesitated, hoping the words were true, and then I glanced to Baylie. "You have your cell?"

Her head shook. "It's on the coffee table at home." She paused, trembling. "What's left of the coffee table."

I reached out, squeezing her hand. She tensed, her gaze flicking to my forearm.

Uncomfortably, I let her go.

"So I guess that's part of the..." she tried in a whisper.

I gave a small nod.

She let out a breath. "C-can I..."

I paused, and then let the spikes emerge.

She tensed all over again, staring at them. Her hand moved toward me.

I pulled my arm away. "They're sharp."

Baylie managed a nod, lowering her hand. She swallowed hard as I drew the spikes back in.

"Guess that's why Noah's skin goes all..." Her fingers fluttered illustratively. "If he's supposed to... you know."

I looked away. I hadn't really thought about it.

I wasn't sure I wanted to.

"What happened there?" I asked, twitching my chin toward her arms.

She shrugged a bit. "Noah's cousins."

It was hard to know what to say. My brow furrowing, I glanced toward Zeke. Sitting on a desk by the windows, he studied the street around the edge of a curtain.

In the distance, police sirens began to howl.

I shifted my weight nervously. I wanted to be comforted by the noise. By the prospect of people with guns getting between us and Earl.

But I knew bullets didn't stop greliarans.

I swallowed, trying not to worry about Noah or Sandra.

"You think they're alright?" Baylie asked quietly.

I glanced to her, seeing the same fear in her eyes as I knew was in mine. "Yeah," I whispered back, doing my best to sound encouraging. "They–"

Zeke made a tense sound, cutting me off. I looked over at him. Barely breathing, he eased back from the window, his gaze locked on something outside.

I crossed the room to his side and peered past the edge of the curtain.

Earl was standing in front of the school.

I froze.

Breathing hard, Earl scanned the street and the school building, his head twitching back and forth in quick, savage movements. His skin was human again, and his eyes were as well, but a snarl curled his lip and I could see him shaking while his fingers spasmed into shapes like claws.

The sirens grew louder. At the end of the block, a police car whipped around the turn.

Earl's gaze snapped toward it. Spinning fast, he took off running down the street.

I let out a breath, leaning closer to the window. They had to catch him. Somehow, they had to–

Another cop car flew around the corner ahead of him. In a screech of tires, it came to a stop and the two officers scrambled out, grabbing for their guns as they moved. The police shouted at him, their words muffled by distance and the thick glass of the windows.

Earl skidded to a halt. I saw him pause, as if evaluating what to do, and my heart climbed my throat.

Carefully, he put his hands behind his head and lowered himself to the ground.

The officers rushed toward him. Kicking Earl's legs apart, they patted him down quickly for weapons and then set to cuffing his hands.

I shivered as they hauled him to his feet and started for the car.

"Come on," Zeke said softly, taking my arm.

Earl's gaze snapped toward us and his face contorted with rage. With a furious shout, he yanked the handcuffs apart and twisted in the officers' grasps. The cops stumbled away, driven by his thrashing. He raced for the school while they fumbled at their belts.

Tasers caught him in the back.

Howling, he crashed to the ground. The cops surrounded him again, and struggled to drag him to his feet.

Zeke pulled me from the window while the police shoved Earl into the rear seat of the closest squad car.

"Is he gone?" Baylie whispered, still waiting by the classroom door.

"Cops have him," I answered tightly.

Air left her. She tugged the door open and hurried into the hall.

I jogged after her, trying not to worry about what we'd find at her house.

The squad cars were the first thing I saw.

We ran around the corner to our street to find almost all of the handful of police vehicles that existed in Reidsburg parked in front of Baylie's home. Two officers stood in the yard, watching the road, while others strode in and out of the front doorway. My parents huddled on their porch, not coming closer to the chaos and eyeing it all like they were afraid someone would think it was related to them. Along the length of the street, neighbors milled about, though a few intrepid ones were interrogating the cops for answers to what was going on.

At the sight of them all, Baylie gave a gasp and sped up, racing for her house.

Zeke and I followed.

"Where is she, then?" I heard Sandra shouting from inside. "You say you have him. Well, where the hell– what?"

Baylie's stepmom rushed out the front door, shoving aside one of the officers who'd been slow to move out of her way. A white bandage was taped to one side of her forehead and her blonde hair was disheveled, but otherwise, she seemed okay.

In a scramble, she descended the porch steps and then caught Baylie when she raced into the yard.

"Oh God, honey, are you okay?" Sandra asked desperately. "Where were you? Did he hurt you?"

I slowed, searching for Noah.

He came to the front door as well, and relief flashed across his face when he spotted us on the opposite side of the street.

I paused, fighting the urge to let my eyes change just to see more clearly if he'd been injured. He didn't look hurt from what I could tell, which was shocking considering the noise that'd been coming from the house when we ran.

But then, he was greliaran. That obviously counted for something.

"*Chloe?*" Sandra cried.

I froze as every police officer and half the neighbors on the block suddenly turned toward me and stared.

Mom and Dad hurried for the steps, their intent to hustle me back into the house as fast as possible abundantly clear.

Sandra got to me first.

"Chloe, honey," she said, grabbing me into a quick hug. Pushing me away again, she scanned me up and down in shock. "Where've you been? What happened?"

"I, um—"

Mom reached us. Her face tight, she inserted herself between us, almost physically pushing Sandra away as she took my arms and began pulling me with her. "Chloe, come back to the house. We—"

"Linda?"

Mom turned, her hands tightening painfully on my arms.

Police Chief Reynolds walked down the steps from Baylie's porch. As he started across the yard, he scanned his officers and the bystanders and us with a pleasant expression.

Except his eyes, anyway. Those were all cop.

A shiver ran through me. This was madness. We no sooner avoided Earl than another threat appeared, this time in the form of a landwalker policeman who might just try to hurt or kill me if he found out what I was.

And who would insist on knowing everything about the past week of my life.

My heart raced as two more officers followed the chief from the house. Handcuffs and guns hung at their belts. They were nearly the size of Earl.

I wanted to turn and run.

"I see your girl's home, Linda," the chief commented mildly as he came up to us. "Can't tell you how happy I am to learn that."

Still hanging onto me, Mom didn't move. An answering smile twitched across her face like a trapped animal. "Yes, well," she managed. "We were just going to call—"

She cut off as Dad hurried to her side.

"Bill," the chief said with a nod.

Dad gave a tight jerk of his head in response.

Chief Reynolds' gaze swept me, Zeke, and the neighborhood in quick succession and I couldn't read anything from his blue eyes. "If it's alright with you, Sandra, I'm going to leave a few officers here and head back to the station now. Your problem is already down there being locked up as we speak, so you shouldn't have any more trouble."

She nodded.

"Love it if you all would join me," he continued to my parents.

Dad made a hedging noise. "We need to—"

"Folks around here are going to have a fair number of questions, Bill," the chief interrupted smoothly. "Might keep them from bothering you and your girl just this minute if they know you're down talking to us."

Mom swallowed hard, glancing to Dad. He hesitated a moment, and then gave another tense nod.

"We'll follow in our car," he said.

The chief smiled. "Sounds good."

I stared as the chief walked away. "You guys—"

"Come on," Dad interrupted.

He headed for the garage. Shifting her grip to clutch my wrist, Mom did the same, bringing me in tow.

Her fingers felt like a vice. Without any option but to follow, I stumbled after her toward the car.

Zeke's hand held mine as Dad pulled the car into a parking space beside the squat brick building that housed the police station.

I couldn't stop trembling. It wasn't like in Nyciena. I knew that. It wasn't even close. No one had shackles that'd shock me, and the cops couldn't get away with beating me up like the Sylphaen had done.

But I still felt terrified. They might figure out that I'd stabbed that EMT. Or poke holes in the cover story my parents had made me memorize again on the way over here.

They might do anything.

And the chief was a landwalker. If he found out I was half dehaian...

A squad car stopped in a reserved space near the front of the narrow strip of parking lot beside the station. Sandra's car, with Baylie and Noah inside, pulled past to take a spot next to us.

"Don't forget what we said," Dad repeated, turning around in the driver's seat. "Blame it on that crazy man. Say he took you. We'll be right there, and anything you don't want to answer, just say you don't remember."

I didn't respond, not taking my eyes from the squad car. The chief climbed from the passenger side while behind the wheel, an officer turned off the engine.

"Chloe."

I blinked and looked at Dad.

"This'll be over soon."

I hesitated. I could see the nervousness on his face. Mom's too. They looked as on edge as I'd ever seen them, and that wasn't helping me in the least.

Tightly, I nodded. We got out of the car. Mom and Dad went ahead of me as I followed the chief around the corner of the building.

The chief's nephew, Aaron, rushed out of the front door and nearly ran into us.

"Chief?" he stammered, a harried look on his face. "I just heard the– oh, hi folks."

He swallowed, his gaze flicking back and forth across the others but continually coming to land back on me. "H-hey, Chloe. How are you? Or, I mean, um…"

Aaron floundered, and I had no idea how to respond.

"Excuse us, Officer Erlich," the chief said placidly.

"Do you want me to call someone, sir?"

"Just get the paperwork ready."

Aaron nodded. "Okay, yeah. I'll…"

He trailed off as Chief Reynolds moved past him and one of the other officers pulled open the door. With Aaron still staring at us, we followed the chief inside.

A small waiting room lay beyond the glass door. Three metal-frame chairs with fake leather padding crowded the walls of the tight space, while a small chrome table took up one corner. A sad-looking plant sat in the other corner, sagging into the speckled tile floor. To the left of the doorway, an opening in the wall revealed the dispatch officer – a middle-aged and heavily set woman that I vaguely recognized from seeing her around town.

"Gladys," the chief said to her as we came in. "Could you get these folks anything they need? And have Smith make the appropriate calls. He'll know what needs doing. We'll just be back here talking for a few minutes."

She smiled at us and then rose from her seat, pausing only long enough to push something beneath her desk. A buzzing sound came from the brown door leading to the remainder of the station.

"This way," the chief said.

I glanced back at the others. I could see the tension on Zeke and Noah's faces, and the outright worry on Baylie's.

"We'll all be here waiting for you," Sandra assured me with a smile.

I couldn't respond. With Mom and Dad, I headed after the chief, and tried to ignore the officers who came behind us.

At the end of the narrow hall, Chief Reynolds led us into his office. A cluttered wooden desk took up half the space, reports and folders covering its top while a computer monitor rose like an island from the paper sea. Diplomas, commendations, and family photographs alike hung on the walls, while on the crowded shelving at the far end of the office, everything from books to Little League trophies filled the space.

He motioned us toward the chairs in front of the desk, and then glanced back to follow my gaze to the shelves.

"The Reidsburg Comets Little League team," he explained. "I coach them during the summer."

I tried for a smile and mostly failed.

He didn't seem to notice as he sank into his desk chair, the springs squeaking a bit under his weight.

"So can I ask Gladys to get you folks anything to drink? Coffee, maybe?"

Mom and Dad shook their heads. He smiled again.

"Alright then." He pulled open his desk drawer and then drew out a small digital audio recorder. "Now, Chloe, I want you to know that I'm going to be taping our conversation, but that's not because you're in any trouble. You're not. It's just to help minimize the chance you'll have to go over things again later, okay?"

I shifted a bit in the chair. "Okay."

He pushed a button on the recorder and then set it down on the desk between us. Leaning forward a bit as though making sure the microphone could hear him, he listed off his name, rank, and the date, and then looked back up to me with a smile.

"Could you give your full name and birthday for the record?" he asked.

I did.

He smiled again. "Thanks. So Chloe, it looked like you were with your friend, Baylie Mitchell, this morning. Were you at her house when the break-in occurred?"

"Yeah."

"Can you tell me where were you before that?"

I hesitated. I was shaking so hard, and I needed to stop. Focus would get me through this because, really, it wasn't that bad. As long as I didn't say anything about, well, *anything*, this would be fine.

Trying to believe myself, I drew a breath. "At home."

He paused briefly. "At home," he repeated as if trying to be clear. "And how long had you been at home?"

I looked to my parents, and then gave a tiny shrug.

"You don't know?"

"A while," I allowed.

"About how much of a while?"

I gave another shrug.

He glanced to my parents. They didn't respond. I wasn't even sure they were breathing.

His brow flickered down and then he returned his attention to me. "So how did you get home?"

I kept my gaze from going to Mom and Dad. They'd made me memorize this.

"My parents picked me up on a road."

He paused. "What road?"

I shook my head.

His eyebrow raised and his gaze twitched to the recorder.

"I don't know," I said.

"How did you end up on this road?"

"I left the gas station and walked down it."

"Gas station?"

I gave a tight nod. "I called Mom and Dad there. I don't remember where it was. I… I woke up in a barn. I walked to the station and called them. They came and got me on the road."

He paused again. "This barn. Where was it?"

"I don't know."

"Okay. Try describing the surrounding area to me. What did you see when you left?"

I worked to keep breathing while I fumbled after the most general description I could think of. "Fields?"

"What kind of fields?"

"I don't know."

"Were there any other buildings nearby? Any vehicles, trees or other things you noticed?"

I shook my head.

His brow furrowed curiously. "No, or you don't remember?"

"I don't remember. It's... it's all a blur."

"Any sounds around you? Maybe smells?"

I shook my head again. "I don't remember."

He nodded. He glanced back to my parents, both of whom were watching us intently.

"Okay," he allowed. "We can get into that more later."

He paused again, longer this time, while he scribbled something on the notepad nearby.

My gaze tracked the pen across the page. I wondered what he'd felt the need to write down.

"Now, Chloe," he said when he looked up again. "I want you to know you're safe, alright? Whatever happened, you're safe here now."

I shifted in the chair again.

"Had you seen the man who broke into Baylie's house before?"

I gave a small nod. "Yeah."

"Was he the one who took you in California?"

"H-he, um…"

I trembled, the words feeling stuck in my throat. Mom and Dad had drilled me on this in the car, while Zeke squeezed my hand and wouldn't meet my eyes. I was supposed to blame Earl. I was supposed to say that he'd taken me from the ambulance, drugged me, and that I didn't remember anything till I woke in a barn.

But I felt like it wouldn't matter. Like the whole story they'd insisted I memorize was such a pathetic bunch of lies, a child could see through them.

And like Chief Reynolds already had, with the way his blue, Santa Claus cop gaze just wouldn't look away from me. Earl had attacked me, it was true. He'd left the bruises that were throbbing in time to my racing heartbeat right now.

But if I blamed him, the rest of it could come out. The part about his daughter dying. The reason he'd wanted to kill us in the first place. As a greliaran, he might believe he had as much to lose as anyone from letting that information out. But he might not. He might start raving about dehaians.

He might let the chief know what I really was. What Zeke was. And Noah.

And everything.

"I don't remember," I whispered.

Mom shifted in her seat. The chief's gaze flicked to her before snapping back to me.

"That's okay," he assured me. "But I want you to know, I mean it when I say you're safe. No one can hurt you anymore."

I managed a jerky nod, even though the words were totally wrong.

"Where had you seen him?"

"I don't know."

"What about the ambulance? Was it there?"

"I don't know."

He paused. "Alright, we can get back to that. Let's talk about the ambulance for a minute. Is that okay?"

I didn't move. That was the last thing on earth I wanted to discuss, short of what I was or where I'd actually been for the past week.

"Chloe?"

"Okay," I whispered.

"What do you remember? Anything the ones inside it said? Perhaps something strange about the way they spoke? Accents? Words they used? Names they might have mentioned?"

My heart felt like it would climb up my throat. Why did he want to know that? Did he know they were dehaian? Sylphaen?

I looked to my parents frantically. "W-why—"

"How is that relevant?" Dad interrupted.

The chief glanced between us. "Well, if the man today wasn't connected to this, then we need any other leads we can get. Speech patterns could help us figure out where they were from. Narrow down the search. Names... well, that's obvious, isn't it, Bill?"

Clearly frustrated, Dad glanced to Mom, whose hands were white from clenching them so tightly. She gave him a helpless look.

"I don't remember," I said.

"The other EMTs on the scene said one of the men escorted you and Baylie back to the ambulance. What did the man say to you?"

"H-he just asked if he could help us."

"What did his voice sound like? Midwestern? Southern?"

I shivered. "I don't remember."

He studied me for a moment.

"Did his voice remind you of anyone? Like an actor, or maybe someone from the radio?"

"I don't remember."

His mouth tightened again.

I trembled harder. I wanted to just say no one took me. I wanted to end this and get out of here. I knew that wouldn't actually finish anything, but I almost didn't care.

Helplessly, I looked to my parents.

"Okay, that's enough," Dad announced, putting a hand to the desk like he was going to turn off the recorder himself. "She doesn't remember."

The chief didn't seem perturbed. "It's important that she try, though." He looked to me. "It's okay, Chloe. You're safe

140

now. You—"

"I said she doesn't remember."

Chief Reynolds paused. His gaze flicked from my parents to me and back.

He reached out and turned off the recorder. Slowly, he drew a breath.

"Two teenage girls are dead, Bill," he told Dad quietly. "Someone in California attacked your daughter in broad daylight, and then two more men tried to kidnap her and Baylie only days after that. Now those guys are dead too. I understand you want to protect Chloe. She..." He paused, his gaze returning to me briefly. "She could have been hurt just by going out west like that, even without everything else that came after. But we need her help now. If it wasn't the man we have in custody, then whoever took her from the ambulance is presumably still out there. And she's going to have to remember eventually.

"There's a lot coming down on you folks," the chief continued. "I know that. And I know it's just going to increase. In the next few days, there'll be a number of authorities who'll need to speak with Chloe, and you both too. She'll also have to be checked out medically to make sure she's not injured and that nothing else bad happened to her. We'll have a psychologist in from Kansas City to help you through all that, and – one neighbor to another – I'll see what the town can do to help with any long-term needs in that regard as well. But we're going to have to track down where Chloe was kept and what happened in the time she was gone. That's important for us, but it's important for her too, so she can get through this. And keeping Chloe from talking to us isn't going to–"

Mom let out a desperate sound.

The chief glanced to her and then looked back to Dad. "I can help you all. I know there are… special considerations here. Things that might have made it hard for Chloe to feel quite up to thinking straight in a place like California, or for some time after. But to do that, I need you all to be honest with me. Let Chloe tell me what she really remembers, and where she's been this past week." He paused. "I want to do what I can to protect her too, Bill."

Still trembling, I watched Dad. I needed a way out of here. My arms kept threatening to sting, and only by making myself keep breathing did I seem to be able to hold the spikes at bay.

But I should have gone on running. Stayed away from here and everywhere else.

Though really, that wouldn't have kept some cop from stopping me on the street and making this all happen anyway.

My stomach wanted to twist into a pretzel at the thought.

"We don't want any trouble here," Dad said carefully. "We just want to go back to our lives like they were."

The chief's mouth tightened. "I understand. But that's going to be mighty hard, Bill, just burying this. I know you could try. But the FBI, the sheriffs here and in California… they're all going to–"

"But Chloe doesn't remember anything," Mom protested,

still clenching her hands in her lap.

He paused. "That might be true, Linda. And maybe she will."

His gaze returned to me and I couldn't look away from his eyes. He knew I was lying. I was sure of it.

"I want to help you, Chloe," he said. "I–"

The door swung open behind us.

I jumped a mile.

Spikes rushed out of my forearms.

Mom and Dad both moved to block any view of me, trying not to get cut in the process. Frantically, I tucked my arms to my sides and fought to draw the spikes back as fast as I could.

Chief Reynolds surged to his feet angrily as his nephew came in holding a clipboard. "Aaron, what the hell are you–"

The chief caught sight of my arms just before the spikes disappeared again.

"Sorry, Chief, I had the paperwork–"

"Get out, Aaron," he ordered, not taking his eyes from me.

"I-I didn't mean–"

"Get *out*, Aaron!"

The door shut as Aaron retreated. Shaking hard, I didn't look away from Chief Reynolds.

He sank back into his chair, still watching me. "Now that's, um… not something I expected."

I swallowed hard.

The chief glanced from me to my parents. "Anyone want

to explain what I just saw here?"

Dad's mouth tightened. "Chloe…" He seemed to struggle to make himself say the words. "Her mother was my sister, and her biological father… he was…"

He trailed off with a grimace.

The chief read between the lines anyway. "And I'm going to guess that's involved in what happened last week?" He paused. "What *actually* happened?"

My parents didn't respond.

Exasperation flickered across his face. "Bill. Linda. Please. I… I realize why you probably hid this. It's not exactly something you can discuss on tape. And besides that, you've heard the same stories I have, yeah? What some folks might do to a child in Chloe's position. But I can assure you, that's not a concern here." He paused again. "Unless that's why people have been after you?"

He directed the last question to me.

I hesitated.

"You're safe, Chloe," he repeated. "So please, is this why people have tried to hurt you?"

I swallowed, wishing I knew whether I could trust the words. "Not exactly."

His brow drew down. I shifted uncomfortably in the seat.

"There's this, um, cult. Of dehaians. They," I glanced to Mom and Dad, "they think I'm some kind of monster. They were trying to kill me. S-sacrifice me, actually."

His brow rose again. "Sacrifice."

I nodded. "They came after us at the cabin. Shot Dad." I twitched my head toward the sling on his arm. "And then some others pretended to be EMTs. They took me and Baylie. Knocked her out, held a knife to her to keep me quiet, and then... and then injected me with a drug. Made me change like one of them, so I... I had to get, you know, underwater or I'd..."

Fidgeting, I trailed off. It felt weird to tell someone what'd happened. Someone who was only slightly less than a stranger, anyway.

"That's where I was this week," I finished uncomfortably.

He didn't say anything for a moment. "And so the one with the odd stab wounds..."

Blinking, I dropped my gaze to my lap. "It was an accident. He had the needle. He was trying to stick it in my neck."

The chief drew a breath and then let it out slowly. "Okay." He glanced to my parents. "But this cult, they're not going to be coming to Reidsburg. They'll stay in California?"

I nodded.

"So we'll just focus on keeping you safe around here. If that man today wasn't related to this, then we just need to make sure—"

He cut off when I made a small noise. "What?"

"There... there is one other problem."

He waited.

I shifted in the chair, trying to figure out what to say since I didn't want to bring up Noah, what he was, or risk my parents letting slip anything about the same. "Earl is connected to this. He's part of a… a group. They hunt dehaians. To, you know, kill them. On the way home, I ran into him. But there are others who followed me back here too."

"Chloe, you didn't tell us this," Mom protested.

I hesitated. "Sorry."

The chief watched me. "Do you know where these others are?"

I shook my head. "They were in a maroon SUV, though. There's five of them. They were at Baylie's house yesterday."

The chief's brow rose. "Them?"

I nodded.

"And the man who broke into the Mitchell's today was with them?"

I hesitated. "I think they know each other."

"Have those other guys tried to hurt you? Threatened you? Baylie's family is pressing charges after how those boys roughed her up, but if there's something they've done to you that we could use to be rid of them even faster…"

He left the idea hanging. I shook my head.

"But your–" Mom started, her gaze going to my scarf.

"That was Earl."

An incredulous gasp escaped her as she looked away.

The chief's gaze went between us. "What are we talking about here?"

I grimaced. My fingers pulled down the edge of the scarf.

His brow rose again.

"He tried to strangle me."

The chief regarded me for a moment, his gaze going between my face and my neck, and then he appeared to push aside whatever had gone through his mind.

"Why don't you go back down the hall to your friends, Chloe?" he suggested. "Your parents and I… we need to talk."

I hesitated, glancing to Mom and Dad. "Um, okay…"

Dad gave me a small nod. Tugging the scarf back into place, I rose to my feet.

"Chloe," the chief added when I reached the door.

I looked back.

"Really glad you're home."

I managed a smile. Nervousness still twisting my stomach, I left the office.

9

ZEKE

The clock on the wall was the loudest thing in the room.

On the chairs beside the front door, Chloe's friend Baylie sat next to her stepbrother, Noah, while on the sole other chair in the room, his mother read a magazine. Behind a window to the next room, Gladys, the middle-aged woman who'd offered us all sodas and candy from her office, now studied something on her computer screen. Meanwhile, I leaned against the wall nearby, too edgy to sit down even if there had been a seat to take and struggling to keep myself from pacing.

Chloe hadn't had the chance to tell the others that the older policeman and his nephew were landwalkers. Or that, if they found out what she was, they might try to hurt her.

Like almost everyone else.

It was infuriating. My 'get Chloe to safety' plan wasn't exactly going according to plan. In fact, it'd gone merrily to hell at every turn. From bringing her to Nyciena to getting her home now, there always seemed to be *somebody* waiting for their chance at her.

I was beginning to think taking her to the Arctic Circle was the only solution. At least it'd get her away from everyone who wanted her dead.

Among other things.

My gaze flicked to Noah. I pulled it away again. He didn't matter. Not where anything besides Chloe's safety was concerned.

Though in my book, there was a good chance that meant safety from him.

I shifted position on the wall. He'd helped us escape from Earl. I appreciated that. But his kind had been created to kill us, and most of them seemed pretty damn obsessed with it. Even if he claimed not to be like them, I wasn't sure I cared. It still didn't exactly make him the type of person you wanted to keep around.

And I was really tired of Chloe having people who might decide they wanted her dead around.

A click came from the handle of the hallway door. I shrugged away from the wall while Noah and Baylie both straightened.

Chloe came out.

She looked pale. Shaken. With a tight smile to Gladys, she let the door shut behind her.

But as she started across the room, she suddenly paused. Her gaze twitched from me to Noah, an uncomfortable look flickering over her face.

"Hey there," Noah's mom said encouragingly as she set

her magazine aside. She rose and motioned for Chloe to take her seat.

Chloe crossed the small space quickly and sank into the chair. "Thanks," she murmured.

"What happened?" Baylie asked nervously.

Chloe glanced to Noah's mother and the woman behind the window. "It... it was fine."

Her voice sounded like it'd been anything but.

I studied her as she sat there, not quite looking at any of us while obviously uneasy thoughts made her brow twitch down. I wanted to press for more, to find out if he knew about her, if she thought he was dangerous, or more specifically if we should be getting the hell out of here right now, but there wasn't a way. Noah's mom hovered nearby, while through the window, Gladys was watching us all with an expression of equally maternal concern.

We couldn't exactly bring up dehaians and landwalkers.

"You okay?" Noah's mom asked. "Can I get you anything?"

Chloe hesitated. "A pop would be nice."

The woman nodded. She headed for Gladys.

Chloe watched her go, and then looked to me. "He knows," she whispered.

A breath pressed from my chest. "Do we need to leave?" I responded, my voice equally low.

She gave a tiny, helpless shrug. "I'm not sure. He said he understood why Mom and Dad, you know, let him believe the other thing. And he doesn't seem like he–"

Chloe cut off as Noah's mom came back. Taking the can, she managed another tight smile. "Thanks, Sandra."

"Of course."

Opening the can, Chloe didn't say anything else. She sat there, not taking a drink, with her fingers wrapped around the metal.

I drew a breath and looked back to the hallway door. She might be right, but I wasn't happy taking chances like this.

In her chair, Baylie shifted position and my gaze flicked to her. On the opposite side of the small room, she and Noah were both watching us, wary curiosity on their faces.

"So Chloe, I was thinking," Sandra said into the quiet. Chloe glanced up at her. "If it works for your parents, I'd like to have you and your family over for dinner tonight. Maybe just some pizza, salad, that sort of thing? Or we could come to your house, if that'd be more comfortable for you?"

Chloe gave a small nod. "Dinner would be great. Thanks."

Sandra smiled.

Silence fell over the room again. The clock kept ticking on the wall.

The hallway door opened. Chloe's parents came out, the older policeman behind them.

They looked tense.

But then, for them, I was starting to suspect that was normal.

While the cop stopped by the window to talk to Gladys, Chloe's parents headed for the exit as though they couldn't get out of the station fast enough.

"Chloe, come on," Bill called.

Eyeing them warily, she set the can aside and rose to her feet.

Bill and Linda were already on their way out the door.

"Bye, folks," the cop said as we followed them. "I'll be in touch soon."

Linda paused and looked back. "Goodbye," she replied, an anxious smile hovering around her tight mouth. "And thank you."

He nodded.

My brow drew down warily, but with that, she just hurried outside.

Sunlight glared in our eyes after the artificial light of the station. In a silent group, we walked around the corner to the cars, with Sandra the only one of us who didn't look distracted or anxious as hell. Noah and Baylie were scanning the area around us, presumably keeping an eye out for his cousins, while Bill and Linda just seemed on a mission to get us out of there sooner than yesterday.

"Guys, what's going on?" Chloe asked nervously when we reached the sedan.

Bill didn't respond. "Sandra? Would you all mind watching the house for a few days?"

Curiosity flickered through the woman's eyes. "Uh, yeah. Sure."

He nodded. "Thanks."

"Wait, where are we going?" Chloe asked.

"Chief Reynolds convinced us there are some people it'd be good for you to see," her mother answered. "He thinks they can help you."

"What people?"

Linda hesitated. "We can talk more on the way."

Chloe didn't move. "Are they the people you told me about yesterday?" she asked, choosing her words carefully. "The ones you talked to about stuff?"

"Yes."

She looked to me. "I-I don't want to—"

"Chloe," her dad interrupted. "It's for the best."

She stared at him, as though incredulous of how that could be.

"Who is this?" Noah asked cautiously.

"Um, they're like—"

"Chloe!" her father barked.

She blinked in shock at his furious glare.

"It'd be better for Chloe if she had her friends around, right?" Baylie interjected. "I mean, she's been through a lot and—"

"Honey," Sandra began. "I don't know if—"

"Yeah," Noah cut in. "We can come with you. Follow in Baylie's car."

Linda made a nervous noise, her expression edging toward fear.

My brow twitched down. She almost seemed scared of Noah.

Like she knew what he was.

"This is not your business, young man," Bill said firmly. "Or yours, Baylie. I appreciate your concern for my daughter, but as you said, she's been through a lot."

He motioned Chloe toward the car.

"Why do I need to see them?" Chloe asked.

Bill's glare deepened and I felt my blood pressure rise. "We are *not* going to discuss this here," he stated.

Chloe's gaze flicked to Sandra and then away. "I don't want to go anywhere. I just got here and–"

"This is not a debate!" Bill snapped.

She stopped, a breath escaping her at his tone. I could see her shaking, and more than anything, I wanted to just pull her away from here and leave.

Because protecting her from things didn't just mean glowing behemoths and Sylphaen.

"This is really the best thing for you, Chloe," Linda added, her expression begging Chloe to believe her. "Please just get in the car."

For a heartbeat, Chloe stared at them.

And then, without a word, she turned and climbed into the sedan. I followed, circling the car to the other door and never taking my eyes from her parents as I got in.

Outside, I could hear Bill talking to Sandra, while Noah and Baylie looked to Chloe through the darkened windows. Linda was back to clenching her hands, studying them all and her daughter with an expression like she wished they were already driving away.

Chloe didn't take her eyes from her lap.

I reached over, brushing her leg with my fingers and then taking her hand when she moved it toward mine.

Bill and Linda got into the car, and Bill's face darkened at the sight of me holding Chloe's hand. I met his gaze flatly and, after a heartbeat, he turned his attention to the sedan. No one said a word as the engine started and Bill pulled the vehicle from the tiny parking lot.

I cast a quick glance back. Noah and Baylie were getting into Sandra's car.

The drive to the house was short, and when he parked the sedan in the garage, Bill spared Chloe a look in the rearview mirror.

"Go inside and pack a bag. We're leaving immediately."

She raised her gaze to his reflection. "Why are you doing this?" she asked, the resentment in her voice so tired, she almost sounded as though she didn't expect a response.

And he didn't give her one. "I said go."

He pushed open the door and left the car, with Linda doing the same a moment later.

Chloe let out a breath, and I couldn't tell if she was about to laugh or cry. "Well, that didn't last long."

My brow furrowed. "What?"

"Them. Not being them."

At that, she opened the door.

"Chloe."

She paused, turning her head back toward me.

"You don't have to go," I said. "We could leave. We don't need to stay here if it's just going to be dangerous for you too."

She gave a tiny shrug of futility. "Where else is there?"

"North. The Atlantic. I don't know. The point is, we don't have to be here."

"And what? You'd stay with me?"

"Yes."

Chloe looked pained. Grateful, but pained, and she shook her head. "I can't keep you from your family like that, Zeke. It's... it's not fair. Ina and Jirral and... I just can't." The futile expression returned. "And I don't know anybody anywhere else."

She left the car.

A breath escaped me. Trying to keep my frustration from my face, I climbed out and headed into the house after her.

Bill and Linda were waiting for us.

I tensed, and from the corner of my eye, I could see Chloe do the same. This was ridiculous. They treated their daughter like she was some mad creature they had to control – and, despite their vigilance, could only barely succeed in doing so – and that was when they weren't behaving like she might fall down dead from the simple act of breathing.

It was absurd. In the past few weeks, she'd survived more than they'd probably experienced in their entire lives. She'd done things, gone through things of which they weren't even aware – and which they couldn't ever be told. Because I was beginning to get the gist of this family. They'd just lock her inside the house forever if they knew. Put her in their own version of a box, like the Sylphaen had done. Their coping strategy appeared to go from nonexistent to nuclear without a single stop in between, and I suspected trying to reason with them only accelerated that transition.

I could understand why Chloe kept as much as possible from them. It was her only defense.

Linda headed toward her the moment we came through the door. "Come on," she said. "I'll help you pack."

Distrust replaced Chloe's caution. "Huh? Why?"

"We're in a rush."

"And why is that?"

Nervous frustration colored Linda's face. "Come on," she insisted again. "There are people waiting."

She started toward the hallway, moving to take her daughter's arm as she passed.

Chloe retreated. "What people? Those elder people?"

Linda's lips compressed. She glanced to Bill.

"Yes," Bill said. "Chief Reynolds is going to call them. Tell them to expect us."

"Why?"

"Because it's polite."

A scoff escaped Chloe. "Why are we going to see them?" she clarified bitingly.

Bill's face darkened. He glanced between me and Chloe. "We'll discuss this once we're there."

Chloe stared at him for a heartbeat, and then shook her

head disgustedly and started for the hall. Linda hurried after her.

I watched Bill, waiting for him to attempt to kick me out now that Chloe was gone.

But he didn't say a word. Briefly, he regarded me, and then he headed upstairs as well.

My brow drew down.

Only a few minutes passed before they returned, Linda carrying a small suitcase and Bill hefting a larger one. Chloe looked stressed, coming ahead of them down the stairs and making a straight line to me once she reached the ground floor.

Bill and Linda ignored it. With the bags, they continued on past us and around the corner toward the garage again.

"He didn't try to make you leave?" Chloe whispered to me.

I shook my head.

She gave a preoccupied nod, looking in the direction they'd gone.

"They say anything about why you need to go meet these guys?" I asked.

"No."

Her brow furrowing, Chloe followed them. They'd already loaded the suitcases into the trunk by the time we reached the garage, and while Linda circled around to the passenger side, Bill motioned for us to get in the back again.

We did so. The garage door rolled upward, and then he pulled the sedan outside.

At the house next door, Baylie sat on the steps, while Noah stood on the grass beside her. They watched the car as it backed down the driveway, their gazes locked on Chloe.

Baylie's hand twitched on her knee, her thumb and pinky flexing briefly, switching smoothly to a pointing gesture, and then relaxing again.

Chloe hesitated a heartbeat. Covering the motion with a brush of her hand through her hair, she gave a quick nod.

I kept my face from giving any sign of my curiosity. Something had just passed between them, I knew. But her parents didn't seem to have noticed.

And I wasn't about to risk changing that.

The car reached the street and, with barely a pause to change directions, Bill sent the sedan racing from the neighborhood. Pressed back into the seat by the acceleration, I shifted uncomfortably. Something felt very wrong about this. About how eager they were to suddenly expose Chloe to these people, when they'd apparently spent years doing the exact opposite. It didn't make sense.

And it worried me.

I watched the neighborhood flash by, and then the town, and wished Chloe had taken me up on the offer to leave.

$\curlyvee$ 10 $\curlyvee$

NOAH

I couldn't believe this day.

In the space of a few hours, I'd found Chloe just *standing* in Baylie's living room, had some greliaran *lunatic* break into the house, gotten in a fight with said lunatic, visited a police station where – thankfully – no one seemed to suspect I'd been a part of what destroyed the den, and then watched Chloe's parents bundle her off to the house with the full intent of taking her God-knew-where.

And when it came to that last, there wasn't a damn thing I could do to stop it.

On the banister of the porch steps, my grip tightened. I drew a breath, forcing myself to loosen my hold before I broke something.

I'd wanted to head straight to Chloe's house the moment we got home, but Baylie had cautioned against it. Stationing herself instead on the porch steps, she'd barely taken her eyes from the house and now seemed to just be waiting for something, though she wouldn't say what.

And meanwhile, I was going crazy.

I couldn't figure out what to think. I didn't know much about Chloe's parents – barring what I'd heard from her and Baylie anyway – but the way they'd treated her in the parking lot had left me stunned. I'd never seen that look on Chloe's face before. Speechless. Humiliated. Shaken.

It'd taken a tremendous amount of control not to do something about it.

And that wasn't the only thing…

I removed my hand from the railing entirely. It'd been a week, maybe a bit more, since I held her in the water when she changed for the first time. It'd been days, and not that many of them, since I had to get her away from the beach. It'd been no time at all.

Yet here she was, going around with this Zeke guy, saying he was somehow here because of her. I didn't know what that meant, but I'd seen the way he touched her. The way he watched her. It didn't take a genius to tell there was a whole *hell* of a lot more than friendship going on there.

And it'd been *one damn week*.

My brow furrowed as I closed my eyes, concentrating hard on breathing and on not letting the whole neighborhood see me go greliaran. I had to calm down. Think rationally. My own safety and that of the porch banister depended on it. Yes, it'd been one damn week. One damn week in which I'd probably looked like the craziest psycho this side of the nut-house, in which I'd threatened her, and in which I'd said things that continued to make me feel sick. I'd terrified her. Flat-out *terrified* her.

I still hadn't been able to shake the memory of that fear in her eyes.

So yes. One week. But it was also a week in which she'd come back. Sure, she'd brought him with her, and sure, her shock at seeing me made it pretty clear she hadn't expected I'd be here. But she'd still come back to land. That'd been more than I could've hoped for a few days ago. And when it came to the two of them, I'd only seen what he did. The way *he* watched her and the way *he* touched her.

But I hadn't seen much from Chloe. She'd avoided him at the police station, and her body language... well, it was nearly impossible to read. So I could be overreacting. The guy liked her. Great. That had absolutely nothing to do with Chloe unless she felt the same and, at the moment, I had no proof that was the case.

I just had a knot in my stomach and an almost overwhelming desire to go into that house and do something about every single thing that was bothering me right now.

And that wouldn't exactly be helpful.

Maybe not, anyway.

I opened my eyes, a breath of a scoff escaping me. I'd avoided the cops once today. I didn't need to push my luck a second time.

The sound of the garage door opening brought my thoughts up short. The Kowalskis green sedan pulled out. Through the darkened windows, I could see Chloe. It looked like that Zeke guy was sitting on the other side of her, since there wasn't anyone else for that silhouette to be. Her parents were up front, both of them seeming intent upon the road.

From the corner of my eye, I saw Baylie's hand twitch on her knee. Chloe ducked her head, almost as if nodding, though she could have been simply brushing her hair from her face.

And then they reached the street and her dad took off like he was driving a Formula One race car rather than an aging sedan.

Baylie rose to her feet and started up the steps.

"What was that?" I asked.

"Chloe's going to text. Tell me where they go."

"You guys use sign language?"

"Our own, yeah."

She pushed open the door and headed inside.

My brow rose. Okay.

I followed her into the house. She was gathering her keys and wallet from the table in the hall.

"So if she's going to text you," I said, "then we can follow her."

She didn't glance away from her things. "Yep."

"Baylie."

She looked up. I could see her shaking.

"Are you okay?" I asked.

"Yeah."

She turned toward the stairs.

"Baylie."

She stopped.

"No," she admitted without turning around. "I'm..." A weak chuckle left her, the noise humorless. "I mean, look at this place."

She gestured distractedly toward the scars on the hallway walls where that greliaran had run into them. To the den door he'd torn through and the debris beyond.

"This is crazy," she continued. "It's crazy and it's frightening, but you know what? I don't care. Chloe may be... what she is, but she's also my best friend and right now, she's in trouble. I saw her. I *know* her. She's scared. And her parents..." Baylie shook her head. "I just have a *really* bad feeling about this."

I shifted uncomfortably. She wasn't the only one.

Baylie looked back at me. "I'm going to help her if I can."

I hesitated. I didn't know what they planned, but regardless, I didn't want Baylie involved if there was a chance she might get hurt.

But I also wasn't sure there was a way to argue with her right now.

And she had the car.

"I'm ready when you are," I said.

She nodded. "I'll pack a bag in case we're gone a few days too, and then–"

Her gaze twitched toward the second floor.

"I'll talk to Mom," I said.

She gave me a grateful smile and then headed upstairs.

I followed. In the room at the end of the hall, Mom was sitting on her bed, papers and folders spread in front of her and the cordless phone at her side. Her brow furrowed in consternation, she flipped through one of the folders and didn't look up when I came in.

"Mom?"

She made a frustrated noise as she glanced away from the papers. "I could have *sworn* the homeowner's insurance was in here somewhere."

I hesitated, not sure how to respond. "Listen, Baylie and I are... we're going to follow Chloe."

She paused, and then set the folder down, a sympathetic look on her face. "Honey, I understand that you want to help. Chloe is a great girl, and I know how that must have looked today. Her parents have always been strict with her – too strict, probably – but she's also their daughter, and she's been through a lot. If they think she needs to go somewhere for help, then you–"

"We're not trying to interfere if they're really helping her. We only want to make sure that's what's going on and that she's okay."

Her brow drew down as her expression hardened. "Noah, it's not your place to judge what Chloe's parents think she needs right now. You can't know what that girl might've gone through, being kidnapped like she was."

I grimaced. "I'm not doing that. It's just–"

"I mean it. You need to let them–"

"It's greliaran stuff."

She blinked, her sternness faltering.

I looked away. We rarely talked about the other side of my life. She'd known about greliarans for years, ever since Maddox had first started showing signs of being one as a little kid, and she understood as best she could, but it was still awkward. She and Dad swore it wasn't why they'd gotten a divorce – their problems had gone beyond that – and she'd never been anything but supportive regarding what we dealt with.

But she was human, and until a few months ago, we'd all thought I was too. That even though I had the tall, muscular greliaran build, that'd been the only thing I inherited from Dad.

It'd been so hard to tell her when I found out that wasn't true.

Carefully, she lay the folder down. "Is Chloe a greliaran?" she asked, her skepticism clear. Chloe didn't look a thing like most of us.

I shook my head. "No, she's just–"

"Does this have something to do with your uncle Richard or that man today?"

"Not specifically," I allowed.

"Then what is it, Noah? How is this greliaran stuff?"

I grimaced. "Chloe's… different."

"Different?"

My mouth tightened. I knew what would happen if I told her Chloe was dehaian. Setting aside the obvious questions, Mom worried about that too. We had better control than many of our kind, but she still dreaded the possibility that her sons might kill something, or some*one*, simply because they couldn't stop themselves.

But I wasn't sure there was another explanation to give.

"Dehaian. And her parents aren't. She's adopted. It's sort of a big mess."

She blinked, thoughts running behind her eyes and settling on the one I'd known I'd see. "Noah..."

"It's fine," I insisted. "I've been around her for weeks. Everything's fine. That..."

My brow furrowed in frustration. I should've told her the truth when I came home. I just hadn't wanted to talk about anything.

"That's where Chloe was, Mom. Not kidnapped. I took her to the ocean. I was there when she changed into one of them. And I know her parents are pretty over the top about this, so I'm concerned that... I don't know. I just don't want anything to happen to her."

She paused. "You're okay?"

"Yes."

A breath left her.

"We only want to make sure she's okay too," I said. "Chloe's going to text Baylie so we know where they go, and we'll follow them there. That's it. And if this is nothing...

we'll come straight home, alright?"

Her mouth tightened. "Alright."

"Thank you."

"Be careful."

I nodded.

Without another word, I headed for the guest room Maddox and I used whenever we came to visit. Snagging my backpack from a chair, I paused only long enough to scan the space for anything I might have missed, and then I hurried for the stairs.

Baylie was waiting on the porch, her phone in her hand and her thumb moving absently over it. She looked back when I closed the door.

"Nothing yet," she said.

I hesitated and then sank down next to her.

"She'll text," Baylie assured me.

My gaze on the street, I didn't respond. I just hoped she was right.

The sooner we were going after Chloe, the happier I'd be.

~ 11 ~

CHLOE

Mom and Dad weren't acting like themselves – or rather, they'd inexplicably gone back to acting like themselves after talking to Chief Reynolds, which was a huge change from earlier and it was creeping me out. I didn't know if Zeke had noticed, or if anyone else would at all, but I could see some kind of eagerness in Mom's eyes. Like she was excited about whatever the chief had told her. And Dad just looked as determined as he'd been that night he drove us back from California. Like, come hell or high water, he was going to get us to our destination as fast as possible.

It gave me a bad feeling, like I needed to be running.

Even if there wasn't anywhere to go.

I couldn't leave. Not really. Zeke's offer aside, I didn't know people outside Reidsburg and I couldn't imagine staying on my own would go too well. I'd heard horror stories about life on the streets. I had no interest in being one of them.

And I couldn't keep Zeke away from his family forever.

He needed to get home. Help Ina. Warn Jirral. Niall was still out there and Zeke had probably been here too long already.

So I had to keep going, even if right now, my parents made my skin want to crawl.

We passed a sign for the Nebraska border. Carefully keeping my eyes to my parents and willing them not to turn around, I eased my cell from my pocket.

Baylie had asked me to text and tell her where we went, and from the fact they hadn't taken my phone away, I suspected my parents hadn't noticed the hand sign. We had dozens of such signals, all designed to compensate for Mom and Dad's insanity and used at random in the hopes they wouldn't figure them out. We'd coped for years that way, trying to overcome the times they'd grounded me or arbitrarily decided I had to stay away from Baylie for weeks on end. From sign language to codes we'd leave on our bedroom windows, we had countless systems for avoiding my mom and dad. When we were kids, we'd even created an entire language based on the placement of our various toys on the windowsills.

I was sort of proud of that last one, actually.

Lowering my phone so it would be hidden between my leg and the door, I eyed it askance while I thumbed through the screens to create a text message to Baylie. I was grateful she'd brought my stuff back with her when she left Santa Lucina, and that my parents hadn't decided to take away my cell in the meantime. I'd missed having a way to communicate that was my own, and not just some phone I'd borrowed from a stranger.

And that meant I could reach sane people at times like this.

The correct screen came up and, still watching Mom and Dad, I swiped in a message as fast as I could and then hit send.

I tucked the phone under my leg, where it'd be easy to reach again.

They didn't look back. I glanced over, catching sight of Zeke watching me from the corner of his eye, between glances to my parents as well.

I hid a smile. I didn't know why they hadn't tried to make him leave. Perhaps they'd just been so eager to get out the door, they'd not wanted to stop and argue – though for them, that was odd as well. But I was glad he was still with me, even if I knew he needed to be leaving for home soon.

And even if everything felt weird now.

The thought killed my smile and brought back the dis-comfort I'd felt since the police station. It wasn't Zeke. He was the same as he'd been this morning, last night, and all the days before. It was me.

And Noah being here.

Being the way he used to be.

Pretty much convincing me that he'd never been the monster he seemed.

And that he'd been saving my life when he'd treated me so horribly.

My stomach twisted. I didn't know what to do. I... I hadn't known any of that when things between me and Zeke had changed. I'd thought Noah hated me. I thought everything I'd believed about him had been a lie. And now that it was clear it wasn't... that he hadn't...

I shifted uncomfortably on the seat. I just didn't know what to do. I wanted things with Zeke to be like they'd been.

And I wanted to figure out this weird, raw feeling that surrounded every thought of Noah too.

Miles and fields sped by, not seeming terribly different than anything that'd come before. Around two o'clock, Dad pulled off the highway for food, and dutifully, Zeke and I ate the burgers my parents purchased, though I suspected that like me, he wasn't hungry at all. Several hours later, the Iowa border fell behind us, and gradually all the fields turned to corn. I texted Baylie again.

And the drive went on.

As the clock crept toward seven, Dad steered the car from the highway toward a small town. A large welcome sign covered in civic club emblems sat at the city limit, greeting us on behalf of anyone who was anyone to the Village of Midfield, Iowa. Warehouses with tractors parked outside followed, and then a church or two, and just as we lost sight of the fields around the town, Dad turned onto a residential street lined with old oak trees.

I slid the phone from beneath my leg. Quickly, I thumbed through the screens and got a blank message ready.

Dad pulled into the driveway of a massive, three-story Victorian house. Situated on a broad corner lot, the building looked like a palace trying to pretend it was a house. An enormous, castle-like turret was attached to one corner and rose to a point above the rest of the roof, while a large gazebo stood affixed to the opposite end of the wraparound porch. Stained glass in jewel tones glittered in the windows, reflecting the early evening light, and a fenced widow's walk perched at the apex of the roof like a watchtower for guards. The predominant color was olive green, with white trim and brown accents, and everything from the siding to the bushes around the house's foundation appeared crisp, cleaned and set just-so.

I glanced to the glistening brass numbers on the porch and then typed the address into my cell.

Dad turned off the engine. I hit send and hid the phone.

Mom glanced at me, and in her eyes, I could see that same, strangely eager light. A hint of a smile twitched her lip, and then she buried it and turned back to push open the door. With a quick motion, Dad put the keys into his pocket and got out as well.

I looked to Zeke. Caution clear on his face, he paused and then followed them from the car. I climbed out after him.

We walked toward the house. The street was quiet behind us, and the only sound came from small birds calling in the trees. Every house in the town could have been abandoned from the silence that surrounded them, and I fought the urge to take Zeke's hand, if only for the comfort that touching him would bring.

Dad and Mom climbed the broad steps to the porch. A dark wood door waited for us, with an oval of cut glass running its length and gauzy white curtains shielding the view of the house's interior. With a quick motion, Dad knocked.

Mom glanced back at me. She couldn't hold in her smile this time, the expression all quivering and hopeful and so weird I wanted to turn and run.

And then the door opened.

An old, African-American man stood there, all of five feet tall. Short-shaved white hair surrounded the gleaming top of his bald head and suspenders held up his khaki pants, while his wool, button-down shirt appeared neatly ironed.

"You're here already?" he cried in surprise. "We weren't expecting you for a week!"

I glanced to my parents. They wouldn't meet my eyes.

The little man didn't seem to notice. He shuffled quickly out of our way on slippered feet and treated us all to a smile so happy, it deepened every wrinkle on his considerably wrinkled face. "Oh, come in, come in."

My parents moved past him, leaving me and Zeke to follow.

The man's smile softened when he turned it on me. "Hello, my dear. You must be Chloe. I don't think we've ever met." He glanced to my parents. "Have we met?"

Dad shook his head.

The old man looked back at me, still smiling. "There you go then. I'm Harman Brooks. Do call me Harman. Did you have a good trip?"

I hesitated, feeling a bit taken back. "Um, sure."

"I'm so glad. Come in, come in."

He motioned again.

With a nervous glance to Zeke, I walked through the doorway. A floor of dark hardwood and walls of white plaster waited inside, stretching down a long hallway that ran to the other end of the house. A sitting room was to our left, with stiff Victorian furniture that looked like no one ever used it, and a large library lay to our right. To one side of the hall, a stairway with an ornately carved banister led to the second floor, while the vaguely rosin-like smell I associated with older people filled the air.

"Who's your friend?" Harman asked me.

"This is Zeke," I said.

Harman looked to my parents again. "Is he the one you mentioned to Barry?"

My brow furrowed at the police chief's name. They'd told him about Zeke?

Dad nodded.

Harman shook his head as though amazed, but he didn't say anything else. Reaching up, he took my hand and tucked it into his arm with a little pat. "Well, I can't tell you how glad I am you made it here," he said as he led me down the hall toward the back of the house. "Your parents came by – what was it? Seventeen years ago? Such a long time. Though I guess it's always like that for the elderly. Folks stop by and then go on their way. It's truly nice when they do come around, though."

He looked up at me with a warm smile.

I did my best to return the expression, and then glanced back to Zeke the moment Harman turned away. Caution still on his face, he followed me, while my parents trailed us both from a few yards back.

"They never did say why they were visiting, you know," Harman continued. "All those years ago. I wish they had, but that's neither here nor there. I understand, after all. You really are such a lucky girl, having them."

I didn't know what to say.

We reached the living room, where the chairs were visibly softer and the furniture looked like it'd actually been used. An ancient, boxy television had managed to find a home between the numerous bookshelves on the rightmost wall, and its screen played images of some storm out on the west coast. Several hardbound books were stacked neatly on an end table near an old recliner, and a steaming mug of tea waited nearby. A sun-room stretched off the back of the space, its windows giving a view of the opulent flower garden in the backyard, while on the opposite side, another archway led to the library again.

A squeak like the springs of an old chair drew my attention. Around the corner of the open doorway to the library, a teenage, African-American girl stuck her head out. A multitude of narrow, curling braids hung past her shoulders and her face had an elfin cast to it. Maybe a year or so younger than me, she regarded us all with a guarded look in her strangely tan-green eyes.

Harman saw me glance to her. "My granddaughter, Eleanor. Come on out here, dear."

The girl left the library and walked into the living room, her expression unchanged.

"Eleanor is just a marvel. She's spending her summer helping me transfer my old catalogs and notes into a... what did you call it? A database?"

At his glance, the girl nodded.

"Database," he confirmed. "Amazing thing. I'm a historian, you know. Well, since my retirement, anyway. But collecting the stories and myths from our rather special history is a passion of mine, and of a few of my friends around the country. There's not many of us, though. But Eleanor, she's the next generation. So smart, so dedicated. She's bringing us all into the new century."

He grinned broadly, sharing the expression between me and his granddaughter alike.

The girl's mouth twitched up and she ducked her head as if embarrassed, though the worry didn't leave her eyes.

"Grandpa," she tried in a soft voice, "do you think maybe we could–"

"Ellie," he reprimanded her with a knowing look.

Her mouth tightened and her gaze flicked from me to the television and back before dropping to the floor.

My brow furrowed.

"So how was the ocean, my dear?" Harman asked me.

I blinked, my focus pulled back to him.

"Barry relayed what you told him," he continued with an understanding smile. "I must say, I just can't even imagine…"

His eyebrows rose and fell and he gave a vaguely theatrical shudder.

I glanced to Zeke uncomfortably. "It was fine."

Harman grinned as if I'd spent an hour detailing the whole story. "Amazing," he said, patting my hand again. "Simply amazing."

Shaking his head, he gave an odd sigh, the sound almost regretful. "Well," he continued, leading me to one of the easy chairs. "Have a seat." He motioned for Zeke to do the same on the couch across from me. "Would you all like some tea? Perhaps orange juice?"

I looked to Zeke briefly. "Orange juice is fine."

Harman smiled. I was beginning to think he never stopped.

"Excellent. Such healthy stuff, orange juice. Could you help me with that, Linda?"

Mom nodded tightly. Tension was creeping back into her face and I studied her warily while she followed him toward the kitchen.

Awkward silence settled over the room. By the hall, Dad stood, glancing between the kitchen and us alike. On the couch, Zeke scanned the room as though watching for an attack, while by the library archway, Eleanor fidgeted and wouldn't look away from the ground.

Mom and Harman returned. The old man carried a tray with several glasses of orange juice on it. A plate sat beside them, and in her hands, Mom held a metal canister of tea cookies.

"So I think we've got everything ready," Harman said, setting the tray on a table by the wall behind me.

Eleanor turned and walked out of the room.

My brow furrowed again as she went. "Um, could somebody tell me why we–"

"Chloe," my dad interrupted. "Don't be rude."

I paused, staring at him. "I just want to know why–"

"Here you are," Harman chimed in at my side. He handed me a glass of juice.

I held the drink, not taking my eyes from my parents. Something felt really wrong, even with cheery little Harman.

Dad's mouth tightened and he glanced to Mom. "We think Mr. Brooks can help you with your problem," he told me as he paced across the room to the television. He rested a hand on top of it.

"My problem?" I repeated. I glanced back to Mom, who had opened the canister and was arranging cookies on the plate. At her side, Harman hovered as though supervising their placement.

"Chloe," Dad sighed. "You have people after you because of what they think you are. What he is."

He jerked his chin toward Zeke.

I let out a breath in a scoff and set the glass down on the

end table. "Dad, those guys aren't our fault. We didn't–"

"It doesn't change anything."

I stared at him. "So what does that mean, then?"

Dad grimaced. He glanced to Mom while she circled behind the couch toward his side. "It's just…"

Something stabbed my neck.

Gasping, I twisted in the seat and grabbed at the sensation. Harman yanked a syringe away and retreated. Eyes wide, I looked over to see Zeke start to his feet.

I couldn't warn him. With a quick motion, Mom jabbed a needle into his arm.

Numbness spread through me. I tried to rise, but nothing wanted to respond and every breath felt as though I was lifting weights with my chest. The world warped like a reflection in carnival glass and through the ripples I saw Zeke stumble and collapse onto the couch.

"What…" I gasped at my parents. "What did you…"

"This is for the best, honey," Dad said, his words murky and far away.

I stared at him incredulously.

"Just you sleep, dear," Harman said next to me.

I turned my gaze to him. Everything was swimming. Going dark.

"Don't worry." His face wrinkled into a warm smile. "It'll all be over soon."

12

NOAH

Midfield, Iowa was actually on the moon.

Or at least that's how it felt.

"How much farther?" I asked Baylie.

She handed me her phone without a word.

I checked the map and tried not to swear. We'd been driving for what seemed like forever, following instructions from short texts that contained nothing more than state borders and highways, until finally we'd received a message with an address a few hours ago.

And after that, there'd been silence.

I didn't want to think it meant anything, but that didn't change the worry that was making it hard for me to concentrate. After all, if things were fine, Chloe would have told us. Even if they *weren't*, she probably would have tried to send something too.

But this...

"So what's the plan, anyway?" Baylie asked.

I pulled up the map again. "Find Chloe and make sure she's alright."

"Okay…" she allowed. "But find her *how*? She's gone quiet, and I'm guessing that means they have her phone. And it's going to be late when we get there. If everyone's asleep and we just come pounding on the door–"

"She won't be."

I scrolled through the highways and state roads. There had to be a faster route. Something. Sure, her parents had apparently gone to a town so tiny and remote, the map barely knew it existed.

But there still had to be *something*.

"Um, okay. But if she is… Noah, her parents are *nuts*. If she's not around when we show up, they could call the cops on us before we even get to see Chloe. I'm not joking. We need a plan. Like, a real one. Do we wait till morning if everyone's gone to bed or do we try to–"

"We won't need to. Dehaians don't sleep."

Silence followed. My mind caught up with the words.

My gaze slid to Baylie.

"*Huh?*" she demanded.

"I mean, they don't always–"

"Chloe *sleeps*," she snapped. "I stayed overnight at her house tons of times."

"Yeah," I agreed carefully, "but she wasn't dehaian then. Not like now."

Baylie cast me an incredulous glance before returning her

gaze to the road. "What else don't they do? *Eat?*"

I hesitated. "You should really talk to her."

She gave me another look, this one more angry than anything.

I grimaced and turned my focus back to the map on the phone.

A moment passed.

"Do *you* sleep?"

I looked back up at her. Hands flexing around the steering wheel, she didn't glance my way.

"Yeah," I answered. "We didn't get that part."

Her brow flickered down and then her head moved in a tight nod.

I hesitated. "Anything else you want to know?"

Her gaze twitched to me and away. A heartbeat passed.

"Created," she said.

"Yeah."

"To kill them."

I paused. "Yeah."

"Is that why your cousins are so... you know, crazy?"

"Pretty much."

"But why? I mean, why—"

"We want to kill them," I explained quietly. "We... we feel like we need it."

She didn't move. "Do *you* feel like that?" she asked carefully.

I looked down, trying to decide what to say. I'd grown up knowing that there was a chance I could be greliaran. Knowing that I might have to deal with the same craving to kill dehaians and experience the high their magic provided that Maddox and my dad did. It was why, from the time we were toddlers, Dad had worked with us, trying to preempt those tendencies. We'd done mental exercises. Meditation. Tests designed to push us, just so we wouldn't lose control of ourselves when real stresses arrived. It didn't matter that I hadn't shown any sign of being greliaran till a few months ago. Dad still wanted to make sure I had what I needed so that, if the time came, I wouldn't lose myself to this thing.

He'd saved us, me and Maddox both. He'd believed there was a different way for our kind, no matter what his brother was like. His own father had started it when Dad and Richard were teenagers, and though my grandfather had never been able to fight it quite as much as we had, ultimately even he'd managed to live an almost normal life.

But it didn't mean that part wasn't there.

That I didn't feel it, deep inside.

I'd just discovered something else, same as Maddox and Dad and my grandfather.

"I want other things more," I said quietly.

She hesitated.

"Greliarans don't get to have lives," I told her. "My kind... except Dad and Maddox and me, anyway... they always end up in the middle of nowhere, isolated from humanity. It's their only defense because in most cases, the drive to kill dehaians has made them *so* insane, they can hardly keep from hurting innocent strangers as a substitute – if they even *want* to stop themselves anymore. That's how bad this can be. I mean, you've seen my cousins. Even living where they do, it's a miracle they're not in jail. And they're as crazy as any murderer who's already been sent there."

I shook my head. "I want a life, Baylie. More than I'll ever want to kill a dehaian, more than I'll *ever* crave that rush. Back before I found out that I was like Dad and Maddox, I thought I might not have to worry about it. That I could be like any other human. And now that things have changed, I'll do *anything* to keep from ending up like the rest of my kind. I want to just *live*, and nothing we were made for can compete with having the freedom to simply do that. Nothing."

She bit her lip, staying silent for a moment. "And Chloe?"

I paused. I knew what she was asking.

But she was also my sister, 'step' or whatever be damned, and Chloe's best friend to boot. I had no idea how to reassure her of the degree to which her friend wasn't in danger from me, because *awkward* didn't even come close to describing it.

I wanted to do plenty of things with Chloe. *Killing* her definitely wasn't one of them.

"Chloe's safe," I managed.

She glanced to me.

"I swear," I continued.

Baylie paused, watching me from the corner of her eye. She gave a small nod.

I let out a breath, returning my attention to the phone.

The arrow on the GPS had moved quite a bit while we'd been talking, and now showed us closing in on Midfield.

Finally.

The sun was past the horizon by the time we pulled into the town, though the moon was bright and turned everything to shades of silver and blue. Streetlights were few and far between, and when we turned onto the street of the address Chloe had sent, the lights vanished entirely. Darkened houses lined the road, their yards higher than the sidewalks and separated from them by short stairways and stone-walled drop-offs. Old trees towered above it all, leaving deep shadows within which the house numbers were lost.

"There," Baylie said.

I glanced over to where she pointed. In the driveway of a massive Victorian house, the Kowalskis' green sedan was parked. Most of the lights in the house were off, though a few still shone from the second floor, and the majority of the curtains were drawn. On the steps to the sidewalk, however, an African-American girl sat with her elbows on her knees and her head in her hands.

Baylie pulled over a few houses shy of the Victorian. Pushing open the doors, we climbed from the car and started across the street.

The girl looked up from her hands as she heard us come closer. She was young, maybe only fifteen, and her eyes were a startling shade of greenish tan.

Her brow drew down with caution when she spotted us.

"Hey," Baylie said. I could hear the tension in her voice. "Do you, um... do you live here?"

The girl took a moment before nodding.

Baylie glanced to me. "We're looking for someone," she continued to the girl. "A friend. Her name's Chloe. We–"

The girl scrambled to her feet. "Wait, you know Chloe? You–"

She cut off, her caution returning with a hefty dose of distrust. Swallowing hard, she glanced around. "What'd you come here for?"

Baylie hesitated. "We're a little worried about her."

The girl's guarded expression didn't change. "Why?"

Baylie gave me a quick look again and I could see the same wariness in her eyes that was probably in mine. The girl seemed like she was checking that we weren't enemy spies or something, and it left me on edge. Chloe *still* hadn't contacted us. If something was wrong and this girl was a part of it...

I drew a breath, focusing on staying calm.

"We don't think she wanted to come," I risked saying. "And we're not sure why she had to–"

"You're not?"

I paused and then shook my head.

The girl bit her lip and cast a glance to the house. Nothing had changed.

"Come on," she said, motioning to the shadows of the sidewalk beyond the house.

My brow twitched lower. We followed her down the

block.

"Listen, um, your friend," she tried. "She's… there's special considerations for her, and it sounds like she hasn't said anything, so–"

"She's not human," Baylie interrupted.

The girl paused. "You know that."

"Yeah."

"Oh." She blinked a few times, visibly resetting. "Okay, well, um … in that case, maybe…"

The girl's gaze went back toward the house. Her brow flickered down and she bit her lip again. I couldn't make sense of the debate that seemed to be raging behind her eyes.

"What's going on?" I asked, struggling with the urge to turn around and head straight inside after Chloe right now.

"Can you help her?" the girl asked, looking back to me.

"What are they *doing* to her?" I pressed, my heart pounding.

She trembled. "Something really wrong."

I headed for the house.

"No," the girl protested, chasing after me and grabbing my arm.

I ripped it away before my skin could change.

"Please," she begged in a whisper. "My grandfather… he has a *lot* of security and her parents are watching her too. You'll never make it in there without the police coming."

She drew a shaky breath. "But I can get her out. Just park your car farther down the street and keep an eye on the house. When we come outside, be ready to go."

The girl started past us.

"Wait," Baylie said. "Who are you?"

"Ellie."

"Why are you helping us?" I asked.

She hesitated. "Because maybe old stories can be true."

My brow drew down in alarm. That sounded so like something I'd said to Chloe weeks ago.

Ellie glanced back toward the house. "Now hurry. Please. I'll have her out of there as soon as I can."

Without another word, she ran for the house.

I stared after her.

"Noah?" Baylie prompted.

I blinked, pulling my gaze to Baylie.

"What do you want to do?" she asked.

I paused. There wasn't another option, short of breaking the door down.

"Wait," I allowed. "For the moment, anyway. And have the car ready to get the hell out of this place the moment we have Chloe back again."

13

CHLOE

The world was dark. Thick fog surrounded me, dampening everything. I couldn't feel my body and my thoughts were like eels, slipping away between my fingers when I tried to grab at them.

"...sorry about earlier," came a girl's voice. "Listen, why don't you all get some sleep? I can watch her for a while."

"I'd rather we stayed here."

Mom. Anger rose in me, though I couldn't seem to hang onto the reason why.

"She's going to be out for a few hours yet," the girl said. "Don't worry. If anything changes, I'll come get you."

"Young lady," Dad said. "I appreciate your offer, but her condition is—"

"I know about her condition. Grandpa told me. And about the treatments as well."

There was a pause.

"I think she's going to need you a lot more after she wakes up than now, don't you?"

Another pause followed.

"We'll be right down the hall," Mom said.

I fought to pry my eyes open as footsteps creaked on the floor, moving away from me. My body felt encased in cotton, and about three sizes too big, and nothing wanted to move.

A door shut. I could feel my heart pounding. The floor closer to me squeaked.

Something slid on the thick flesh of my arm, pulling off from it with a pain like an insect bite and then being replaced by pressure a heartbeat later.

"Please be okay," the girl whispered as though to herself. "Please."

My arm lifted and fell as someone picked it up, wrapped something around it and then returned it to a soft surface. A moment passed, and then the entire series of sensations repeated on my other arm.

"Wake up," the girl urged. "Come on. Be okay and wake up."

I wanted to respond. To ask what had happened to me. Her voice was starting to seem familiar, though a weird, panicky feeling came with the recollection.

My heart pounded harder. That feeling was important. Something *had* happened. Something bad. I needed to run.

I had to get out of here.

The panic grew. An ache spread through me, permeating

both the fog and the dense clay my body felt like it'd become.

My eyes opened.

A white blur lay in front of me, and slowly resolved itself into a narrow bed. Pale moonlight streamed through the gauzy curtains of the window to my left, lessening the shadows of the small room. A shut door waited on the opposite wall, with a tall dresser at its side.

I pulled my gaze to the right, finding the old man's granddaughter standing next to the bed.

Relief filled her face. Quickly, she reached for the blanket covering me.

"I'm going to move you, okay?" she whispered while she tugged it aside. "I need you to help me, though. I-I know it's hard, just please do everything you can."

I didn't respond. The ache was building into a burn, like someone was slowly turning up the heat on my skin.

She gave a swift look to the door, and then she took my legs, pulling them to the side and off the bed. Moving quickly, she turned and slid her hands under my arms. With a grimace, she hefted me up into a sitting position.

My hand caught the edge of the bed, bracing me while the world swam. I dropped my gaze to the floor.

"What…" I managed, my voice hoarse and choked.

My words trailed off. I was in a blue hospital gown and cotton shorts, with the back of the shirt left open to the air. On either side of the bed, IV bags hung from metal supports, while tubes ran down to where I'd lain on the sheets.

I looked back at the girl, my brow furrowing in confusion.

She grimaced as she turned from grabbing my shoes off the floor. "We need to go."

"What..."

"I can explain when we're outside," she said as she pushed the shoes onto my feet. "Please, Grandpa or your parents could come back any minute."

Fear and anger kept me rooted to the bed. We'd been having orange juice. My parents and Harman – that was the old man's name. And she was Eleanor – had been making me nervous. And then I... I couldn't remember. Mom had...

An image of Zeke falling flashed through my mind.

I gasped, my eyes going wide. "Zeke. Where's Zeke?"

Her grimace turned to a wince. "He, uh... please, we need to go."

"Where is he?" I demanded, my voice growing stronger.

"Please," she begged in a whisper. "If I don't get you out of here now..."

I stared at her, something in her face making me doubt the wisdom of continuing to ask questions till we were outside like she wanted. Because I didn't know what had happened, but my parents or her grandfather–

His wrinkled face looking down at me. Bright lights behind him. Voices in the distance. Beeping too.

"Chloe, focus."

I managed something like a nod, my heart pounding harder as I fought the memory and the pain away.

With a worried look, she took my arm and looped it over her shoulder.

"Try to support as much of your weight as you can. I'm going to lift you."

I eyed her petite size doubtfully, but worked to do as she said when she struggled to pull me upright. My legs wobbled as I reached a mostly standing position, but after a moment, the shakiness began to pass.

We made our way toward the door.

"Okay, just brace yourself there," Eleanor said, nodding toward the tall dresser to the left of the door.

I leaned on it, trying to keep breathing. The burning on my skin was getting worse.

Eleanor opened the door and peeked outside. She checked both directions, waiting for what felt like an eternity before finally nodding to herself. Turning back, she took my arm again.

We shuffled out of the room.

A plush, Persian-style carpet ran down the hallway, leaving space on either side for the hardwood floor to show, and small sconces on the wall provided dim and golden light. With a look to the closed door at the rightmost end of the hall, Eleanor turned us both and then headed for the stairs in the opposite direction.

Breathing was hard, and motion was too. Sweat broke out on my forehead as we passed another bedroom door and, by the time we came to the steps, I'd begun shaking and couldn't stop.

The stairs stretched below me, ending in an oval of moonlight from the front door's window that swam in and out of focus on the foyer floor. Drawing a breath, Eleanor shifted my arm on her shoulders and then started down.

My stomach rolled with the descent and I swallowed hard as I gripped the banister. I wouldn't throw up here. Or at all, if I could help it. But definitely not here.

The first floor arrived.

"Just a bit farther," Eleanor urged.

It was all I could do to keep putting one foot before the other.

With her free hand, she fumbled open the front door. The cool night air hit me, breaking through the nausea for a moment. I drew a breath in gratefully.

A door opened upstairs.

Eleanor made a tiny, panicked sound. Moving faster, she hurried us outside and looked around frantically.

A car door shut somewhere in the darkness. Eleanor kept going, her breaths coming in short gasps from the effort. Together, we hobbled to the porch steps and started down to the yard.

I heard a cry from the second floor. It sounded like Mom.

My heart climbed my throat. I tried to go faster, though I was shaking so hard it felt like my legs would give out at any moment.

Noah came running toward us.

"Take her, take her," Eleanor pled in a whisper when he reached us.

He didn't hesitate. His strong arms scooped me up and held me tight.

Footsteps pounded on the stairs inside.

Noah took off and Eleanor did as well, both of them tearing across the yard for the street.

A car engine started.

Hanging onto Noah as I bounced in his arms, I looked back to see Mom dash from the house. "Stop!" she cried, racing down the porch stairs. "Let go of my daughter!"

Gripping me tighter, Noah jumped the steps from the yard to the street and kept running. Baylie pulled her car up in front of us. Eleanor yanked open the rear door and scrambled inside. Noah pushed me after her and then followed us in.

Baylie hit the gas.

The car sped away, leaving Mom yelling after us in the darkness.

I sat between Eleanor and Noah, shivers wracking me while I fought to keep from throwing up. Heat burned my skin, sinking into my muscles and growing stronger despite the cool night air rushing through the open windows of Baylie's car.

"What'd they do to her?" Noah demanded. He tugged the back of my hospital gown closed and then wrapped an arm around my shoulders to steady me as Baylie swerved the car past a turn and raced toward the edge of town.

Eleanor didn't answer. Breathing hard through the pain, I turned my head, finding her in the darkness.

She grimaced. "A while back, Grandpa and some other people started developing a way to help kids who are half and half. They give them drugs, gene therapy, all sorts of experimental stuff. The goal is to repress what the kids are so the need to change won't ever come." She glanced to me. "It takes their dehaian side away."

"But she's not like that," Noah argued. "She survived."

Eleanor nodded. "I-I know. But her parents wanted him to do it anyway. They said there were these, um," she glanced between Baylie and Noah, "these people after her and if they learned she wasn't dehaian anymore, they'd leave her alone."

A breath left Noah and he turned away.

I stared at her.

"I'm sorry," she said. "I didn't want them to, but Grandpa…"

She bit her lip.

My brow furrowing, I dropped my gaze to the ground, staring unseeing at the gray carpet and the few bits of dried leaves and dirt there. Mom and Dad had done this. Wanted this. Mom and Dad…

Had brought me here to take who I was away.

And they'd looked so excited about it. They'd nearly run out the door just to drive here. But why not? Sure, there were the greliarans and the Sylphaen now, but before that there'd been years of hiding what I was because they thought that if the other landwalkers knew, they'd try to turn me dehaian.

It must have been Christmas to find out the opposite could also be true.

And that they could finally get the landwalker daughter they'd always wanted me to be.

Rage quivered through the nausea and the pain, making me shake for a whole new reason.

"So… so did they…"

I swallowed hard, barely able to finish a sentence. Noah's arm tightened around me.

"It's a process," Eleanor answered. "It's fairly effective from the first treatment, but it still needs boosters over time. Since you just had the one dose…" The worried look strengthened in her eyes. "You might be okay."

"Might?" Noah growled.

"I-I'm not sure. She's not like anyone else, and…"

Eleanor trailed off, watching me for a heartbeat before her brow furrowed and she dropped her gaze away.

"And it's not just that," she admitted uncomfortably. "Grandpa did other stuff too. He… he's not a bad person. He's a genius, really. But he used to be a doctor, and over the years, he saw a couple kids die. He thought Chloe could help him figure out how to make the treatments better. Keep the ocean from hurting half-and-half kids at all. There's never been someone who's been able to keep a balance between their dehaian and landwalker sides before. Who's changed and

survived and even come back all this way on land. He just...
he didn't take that the same way I do. He knows our history,
but unlike some of the other elders and landwalkers, it's only
stories to him. Things he collects." She paused. "He and his
friends don't want us to be dehaian. This was just the best
chance they'd ever have to study somebody who became one."

"What did he do?" Noah pressed, his voice dangerously
low.

"I-I don't know. I think he took her blood. Maybe tried
other stuff too. He has this laboratory where he created the
treatments for those kids, and he had her there for a long
time, and on those IVs when they brought her back to the
house, so..."

I shivered, my hand clenching on Noah's arm as memories
flashed like camera bulbs in my mind.

"Just please don't do anything dehaian for a while," Eleanor
begged me.

I didn't answer. I could see him. Little Harman, hovering
over me with those bright lights behind him and a smile on
his face.

Lab. He'd had me in a lab, doing this to me while I slept.

I couldn't breathe. Panic gripped me, demanding I run
though there wasn't anywhere to go. There'd been tubes connected to me. Colored liquids inside them. People in the
shadows and voices too muddled for me to understand.

And then he'd noticed I was awake. He'd adjusted something and smiled at me as the world drowned in fog again.

"Chloe." Noah took my face in his free hand, pulling my gaze up to his. "Focus. Stay with me here."

I couldn't respond. His green eyes searched mine, visibly trying to calm me by force of will. And I just couldn't... my whole body was burning from what they'd done to me... to us...

"Where's Zeke?" I rasped, turning back to Eleanor.

She hesitated.

"Eleanor, where's Zeke!"

"I-it's Ellie," she corrected awkwardly. "And I don't know. They took him when they took you. They didn't bring him back."

I stared at her. "Who?"

She shifted uncomfortably. "Your dad and some guys my grandfather works with."

More shudders wracked me. I wanted to cry from the way they hurt. "Where are they?"

"I-I'm not–"

"Where!" I shouted.

Pain stabbed me like spikes in my midsection and I doubled over, gasping. Noah grabbed me, tugging me back upright. I choked, my head falling back to rest on the top of the seat.

"Baylie, stop!" he called.

The car rocked as Baylie pulled over.

I clenched my hands on Noah's arm. My bones felt like they were breaking, like my own muscles and skin were crushing them. I couldn't breathe, couldn't scream, and my stomach kept trying to climb my throat.

Noah threw open the door and hauled me after him as he left the car.

My feet stumbled on the gravel and my legs refused to hold me up. As we reached the scrub grass beside the country highway, my stomach finally won.

Noah got me to the bushes just in time.

Shivers ran through me again as the heaving stopped. His hands on my shoulders, Noah helped me retreat from the ditch and then eased me down onto the edge of the highway. Baylie appeared beside us, a bottle of water in her hand. Quickly, she sank down next to me, pushing the bottle into my grip.

I could barely hold onto it. My hands didn't want to work and I just couldn't stop shaking.

"Where's the nearest hotel?" Noah asked.

I made a noise of protest. We needed to find Zeke.

Everyone ignored me.

"Oak Falls, I think," Ellie answered.

"Tell Baylie how to get there," he ordered.

He scooted around, the gravel scraping beneath his shoes as he moved, and then he lifted me again. The world swirled as he turned and carried me back to the car.

My forehead pressed to his shoulder in effort to stop the spinning. Shifting around, Noah lowered me onto the seat, and then pulled me close as he joined me back there.

The door thudded shut behind him. I heard Ellie climb into the passenger seat. The engine started, and then the car bumped off the shoulder and back onto the country highway.

Tears leaked from beneath my closed eyelids, driven by pain and totally out of my control. The quiet sounds of the car felt loud as foghorns in my mind, and my fingers dug into Noah's chest from the way it all hurt.

But I had to go. The pain didn't matter, because I couldn't lose Zeke like this. I couldn't come this whole way with him only to have some psychotic, smiling monster dissect him. And that was if he didn't just die, all these thousands of miles from the ocean and here because of me.

I had to go. His family needed him. *I* needed him.

And somehow, he had to be alright.

14

ZEKE

Sweat dripped down my back beneath my sodden t-shirt and, stretched out on either side of me, my arms burned from pulling at my restraints. Curved bars of thick steel wrapped over my wrists and pierced through holes in the upright table behind me. My legs were likewise pinned with a single bar, and no matter how hard I tugged, the locks fastening the restraints behind the table's surface didn't budge. Boxy devices on chrome stands waited to each side, with cords coiled on top of them or trailing to the floor, while a metal table stood several feet away. Shelves stretched between the legs of the table, with strange jars of liquid arranged on them.

I wasn't sure how long I'd been here. It felt like hours, but that could be wrong. I'd woken in this place, strapped to this table like I was standing in midair and with a headache that threatened to split my skull. It'd taken a while for whatever Linda had given me to stop dragging me back down into unconsciousness, but eventually the fog cleared.

And brought back the memory of that little bastard jabbing something into Chloe.

My arms yanked at the bars again.

Nothing changed.

I didn't know what they'd done with her. She wasn't here. The room was pitch black and the drug had slowed my body's reactions, but after a minor eternity I'd been able to change my eyes enough to confirm that, at least. Something was going on beyond the door on the opposite side of the room, though. Voices carried through there occasionally, too muffled to understand, but enough to tell me I wasn't alone.

Sweat stung my eyes and I blinked, shaking my head to drive it away. Stuffy didn't come close to describing this room. The reek of oil filled the space, along with an earthy scent not quite like dirt. The walls were metal and, after baking in the sun all day, the trapped heat inside them made my lungs feel like they were working overtime just to pull in the air.

That wasn't the worst of it, though. Not by a long shot. In the past few minutes, a weird, stinging sensation had begun to grow in my body. It was still faint, like a thousand hair-thin needles resting on my skin, but gradually it was getting stronger. I wished I could believe it was just numbness from the restraints or a residual effect of whatever drug I'd been given.

But I remembered this feeling.

The pain of the ocean's distance was coming back.

And I was trying desperately not to think what that might mean about Chloe, or for me.

Hinges creaked in the darkness. My gaze snapped to the door across the room as it swung open. Light cut through the black and I winced, my eyes adjusting too slowly to keep the glare from hurting.

The little old man paused as he saw the glow fade. "Oh, interesting," he commented. "I'd hoped to see that."

With a coffee cup in one hand and a leather briefcase in the other, Harman nudged a switch beside the door. A row of panel lights flickered to blinding life above us. Letting the door shut behind him, he came farther into the room.

Anger sizzled through me. "Where's Chloe?"

"How did you learn English?" he replied curiously.

My brow furrowed.

"I assume you don't always speak that," the old man continued. "I mean, that would just be silly, right? You must have your own language. What is it?"

I blinked, and then pushed my confusion aside. "What have you done with Chloe?"

He studied me as though trying to read something in my face. "Fascinating. Why do you feel the need to portray worry for your thrall? Is it a ploy for sympathy? A tactic to make others see you as human?" He paused, concern flickering over his face. "I *would* hope you'd have the intelligence to see I won't fall for that."

His brow drew down as if the possibility I didn't troubled him, and then he turned to set down his coffee cup and briefcase.

My hands yanked at the restraints.

"To answer your question – because I want us to get past this so you can answer mine – your thrall is safe. Better than safe, actually, since my associates and I are treating her condition. That was what kept me; I do hope you understand. Amazing girl. So much to study, I simply didn't know where to begin. Her body handled the treatments admirably, though, and I returned her to my home with her parents a short while ago. She'll be out until at least tomorrow morning, but when she wakes… well, what we gave her should shake your hold on her quite well. After all, magic may be your people's province but science is mine, and we've long since proven which one is stronger. The treatments will repress those dehaian contaminants in her system and begin to flush them out, and put the young lady well on her way to being her old landwalker self again."

I stared at him.

"My boy, you honestly didn't expect her parents to let her remain like that, did you? Magically enslaved to you and driven to become a soulless water creature as well?" He scoffed, and when he said the word 'water', he made it sound like a curse. "I'll admit, they wanted to be kinder than I'd have been in their position – insisting I send you back to the ocean even after what you did to their daughter. But those are unscientific minds for you. Shortsighted and emotional. Regardless, it's incredible the girl survived. I wish we'd had more time to study that, because there's no telling how many additional clues she could have given us for saving other thralls and half-breeds from death. But the young lady's mind was at stake. Who knows what damage more time as one of you could have done to her?"

Shaking with tension, my arms strained against the metal bars and I couldn't take my eyes from him any more than I could wrap my head around what he'd just said. He'd stopped her from being dehaian? It wasn't possible.

At least, it shouldn't have been.

"You…"

"I wonder if she'll remember you when she wakes up," Harman mused, ignoring me. He shook his head to drive the thought away, and then turned to the table and opened the briefcase. "If she doesn't, it would be interesting to study why."

He turned back to me, a glistening pair of scissors in his hand. I tensed, pulling away as he came toward me.

"Don't move," he cautioned.

Harman reached out, taking the bottom of my t-shirt and then slicing up through it, cutting it from me. Doing likewise with the sleeves, he tugged the cotton away when he was done. Crossing to the table, he bundled the fabric into a plastic bag, sealed the top, and then scribbled something on the side.

"Just in case it's scientifically interesting," he explained as he set the bag down. "Now…"

He headed toward the boxy device on a stand to my left. Drawing up the thickest of the cords from where it dangled next to the machine, he fumbled around on the wall for a moment, trying to plug it in.

The device started to beep. Little lines of red and green ran across the screen on its front.

Ignoring it, Harman pulled a tray on rollers from farther behind me, positioning it at my side. Gauze and rolls of a white material that looked a bit like tape sat on the gleaming silver surface, while scalpels and needles rested on a cloth beside them. Returning to the machine, he took up some of the thinner cords with plastic discs attached to their ends and then came toward me.

I pulled back again, but there wasn't anywhere to go. He tugged a covering from one side of the small, plastic discs and then pressed the discs to my chest, where they stayed.

Numbers appeared on the screen. The lines became zigzags.

I swallowed, looking from him to the machine and back. "What do you want?"

His mouth tightened thoughtfully while he scrutinized me. "Blood first, I think. Good to have a baseline for comparison later."

My heart started pounding harder as he turned to the tray and picked up a syringe. "I said, what do you want?"

He looked up at me, his eyes the picture of innocence. "To study you," he replied as though it was obvious.

I flinched as he jabbed the needle into the inside of my elbow. My blood started to fill the syringe.

"Oh," he commented, his attention on my arm. "I *should*

mention that you'd probably do well to refrain from charming me with that little magical ability of yours. For one thing, I have absolutely *no* intention of letting this opportunity pass me by, so I doubt your magic will do much. For another, my associates are watching us on closed circuit cameras," he nodded to a tiny black device above the door, "and we have an agreement that, if any of us tries to let you escape, we'll be killed on the spot and so will you." He glanced to me. "Security measures, you understand. None of us want to live as a mindless slave."

Harman withdrew the needle and pressed a bundle of white gauze to the place where it'd been. With his free hand, he set the syringe down on the tray and then took up a roll of tape.

"I can't tell you how intrigued I was when I learned the Kowalskis had a dehaian with them," he continued while he adhered the gauze to my arm. "Setting aside how you even managed to travel this far – although I do want to discuss that later and a clear explanation would be best, so please be thinking about it – I've been waiting for *years* to have a dehaian brought to me. But it never worked. They found so few, and when they did, they just couldn't restrain themselves." He shook his head, his attention on the syringe he was labeling. "It's those pesky instincts, you see. They're so driven by them. Like animals, really. They simply can't keep themselves from what they were made for. And so few try. It's rather sad, if you think about it. Or, at least, it is for what I need."

He returned the labeled syringe to the tray and drew a

breath. "But in any case, now we finally have–"

A knock on the door cut him off. His brow furrowing, he glanced back and then crossed the room.

"I asked not to be disturbed," he said as he tugged open the door.

"And we thought we'd have the scale-skin you promised us by now," came the response.

Harman stumbled back as a large man pushed past him. Built like a weightlifter and nearly as huge as Earl, the man scanned me up and down with disgust curling his lip. Four enormous guys with dark buzz cuts followed him, each of them like younger – but only slightly smaller – versions of the man who was obviously their father. More muscles than should have been possible covered their arms and chests, the latter of which were readily visible under t-shirts tight enough to have been painted on.

The four guys started right for me.

I tensed, my heart pounding at what damn near looked like hunger in their eyes.

They had to be the ones who'd been chasing Chloe and me. Noah's family. The math was there, and I couldn't believe five *other* behemoth freaks happened to be looking for a dehaian to kill too.

I pulled at the restraints, cursing internally at the thick metal and the way it had yet to give.

"Hey, hey now," Harman protested, hurrying in front of them. "You don't have any right to interrupt me like this."

The biggest of the four pushed past him with a snarl.

"You offered us a dehaian in exchange for leaving the girl alone," their father retorted. "That gives us all the right we need."

"I offered you a dehaian *after* I was done with him," Harman corrected, still trying to stay in front of the others. "You greliarans haven't been able to provide me with a research subject in all these years, Richard. You have to give me time with this one now."

Glowing cracks spread through the guy's face as he came closer. My hands yanked harder at the restraints and adrenaline pushed the spikes out of my forearms.

"Wyatt!" the man snapped.

The guy stopped.

"Amazing!" Harman cried. He spun toward his briefcase.

I didn't take my eyes from Wyatt. Growling under his breath, he stared at me and twitched as though barely keeping himself from lunging.

Harman grabbed something and then hurried toward me.

Silver flashed at the corner of my eye. I pulled my gaze from Wyatt just in time to see Harman clamp one of my spikes with the device in his hand.

Startled, I tried to pull my arm away and draw the spikes back in. Harman gritted his teeth, fighting me. His other hand came up, holding something that looked like scissors, only the blades were curved.

And quickly, he cut the spike off.

I cried out in pain as my other spikes retreated, the skin sealing over where they'd been. Gasping, I doubled over while my nerves screamed. It felt like he'd cut off a finger. Like he'd sliced straight through bone. All my other senses shrank down on that one spot of agony on my forearm, blocking out everything else.

A hand grabbed my neck, shoving me back upright, while another took my arm, crushing down on the place where the spike had been.

I choked. My eyes opened to see Wyatt's face inches from mine.

"Wyatt!" his father barked.

There wasn't anything sane in the guy's eyes. Nothing human in the least. He gave no sign of hearing anyone as he stared at me and clenched his hand tighter on my arm, drinking in the sight of my pain.

"Stop him!" Harman protested. "Richard, if your kind want our help at *all* anymore, you can't let him kill my dehaian!"

Richard appeared behind Wyatt. Expressionless, he slammed his fist into his son's side.

Wyatt flinched, his grip on me loosening.

"Drop it," his father snapped.

Growling, Wyatt held me for another heartbeat, and then thrust me backward into the metal sheet. Releasing my throat, he turned and stalked back toward his brothers.

Coughing, I watched him and his father equally. Richard studied me, his lip twitching with the same hunger as his son and his eyes just this side of rational. With a disgusted noise, he looked to Harman.

"The deal stands," Richard snarled. "We stay on the coast and bring you one of the scale-skins if we can. You landwalkers use the clout of the people you have in the legal system to our advantage. You try to change that now, there might just be an accident we couldn't save you from."

Harman swallowed, his hands gripping something beneath the edge of the table as if hanging on for dear life. "I only need him for a few hours. After that, he's all yours."

Richard's gaze twitched from the little man to me. "A few hours," he agreed. "And he better be alive for us then."

Without another word, he motioned to his sons and then headed for the door.

"Now!" Richard barked when they didn't move.

Still watching me over their shoulders, the guys filed out of the room after him.

The door closed.

Harman let out a breath. He released whatever he'd been hanging onto, and looked back to me.

"Well," he said as though attempting to calm down. He fidgeted with the placement of a jar of water atop the table. My stomach twisted at the sight of the spike from my arm immersed within. "Let's see what else we can learn, shall we? After all, we only have a short time."

He came over. Taking up another syringe from the tray, this one filled with a blue liquid, he regarded it in the light.

I tugged at the restraints, desperately trying to break the locks holding them closed.

"Now just stay still." He turned to me and lifted the needle toward my arm. "This might hurt."

15

NOAH

On the edge of the motel bed, I sat watching Chloe. She'd been delirious since before we'd arrived, gasping and shaking like she'd run for miles and mumbling things I couldn't understand, and a few minutes ago, she'd finally passed out. Her tears had stopped a short while before that, exhaustion or something else dragging her down till she couldn't cry anymore.

But she was still in pain. So much pain. Even unconscious, she twitched and moaned like she was trying to escape something.

And it only seemed to be getting worse.

"How do we stop this?" I asked, glancing up at Ellie.

Standing across the tiny room with her hands pressed to the faded wallpaper behind her, the girl shook her head. She hadn't taken her eyes from Chloe since we'd reached this little motel on the edge of Oak Falls. "I don't know. They... they tried to make her a landwalker, and–"

"I know that," I said, struggling to keep the edge from my

voice. "What can we do to stop it?"

She shook her head again.

Grimacing, I looked back down at Chloe. Sweat plastered her auburn hair to her cheeks and every few moments, she'd flinch like something was hurting her. On the other side of the bed, Baylie sat, a bucket of ice water on the nightstand next to her and a cold rag in her hand. Over and over, she dabbed the cloth to Chloe's forehead, looking like she was trying not to cry as well.

I took Chloe's hand in mine. I wanted to kill the man who'd done this, Ellie's grandfather or not. I wanted to make him pay for thinking he could just experiment on anyone, let alone a girl who'd already been through so much.

And as for Chloe's parents...

I drew a breath as I felt my skin start to change. That wasn't helpful right now, no matter how good it would feel to let my greliaran side out. To go back there and give them a *damn* good reason for being afraid of me, and for never coming near Chloe again.

The colors started growing brighter and sharper as my eyes changed too. I closed them fast, my fingers tightening around Chloe's hand. I wouldn't be like that. I wasn't like that.

And I needed to focus here right now.

"Noah?"

I opened my eyes at Baylie's voice, looking from her to Chloe to make sure nothing had gotten worse – and noting gratefully that the world appeared its same dull self again.

"You remember after the boat capsized a few weeks ago?" Baylie asked. "What happened when we got home?"

I paused, thinking back.

"She collapsed, remember? We were freezing, but Chloe was all sweaty-looking and then she—"

"Yeah, I remember."

"What if this is like that? I mean, she'd never been in the ocean before, right? And she's..."

Baylie seemed to struggle to say the word. She glanced to Chloe worriedly.

I followed her gaze. This was about a hundred times what'd happened that day, if not more. But it did look sort of similar.

She'd been changing then. She hadn't known it, none of us had, but now that I looked back, I could see the signs. The way she'd just been floating under the water when I grabbed her, not struggling or trying to swim at all. The way she'd been so quiet and shaken afterward.

Of course, the ocean *had* just gone mad and attacked the boat – something I still couldn't figure out – but the point remained the same.

I wondered if she'd been breathing under there. I wondered what she must have seen.

"So what're you thinking?" I asked Baylie, pushing the memory away.

"I don't know. That's when this started, though, right? Or close to. And she was probably becoming one of them when that happened, and then she got better after it so... I don't know. Maybe this is like that, but in reverse. So if we try to push her back toward being one of them..."

She gave a helpless shrug.

"That could kill her!" Ellie protested. "Please, you can't risk—"

"*This* is killing her," Baylie countered heatedly.

"But she could get better if we just let the treatment work its way out of her system."

I looked back at Chloe. She seemed paler now. She hadn't stopped sweating, and something told me it'd probably be bad if she did. Like her system had given up. Or she'd run out of ability to fight this.

"Changing into dehaians kills these half-and-half kids, right?" I asked Ellie. "That's what you called them?"

"Uh-huh."

"Okay, but Chloe survived that. She's not like them anymore. So what if Baylie's right? What if this is pushing her back toward what kills them, rather than fixing anything? And if we can get her to change toward her dehaian side again, maybe it'll stop this."

"How are you going to do that?" Ellie asked. "We're a thousand miles from the ocean."

I didn't answer, returning my gaze to Chloe. We couldn't make saltwater here. Replicating the ocean wasn't exactly as easy as dumping rock salt into a bathtub.

But maybe she didn't need that. Maybe all she needed was a push. Something that felt like it, even a little bit. There were all sorts of things in regular water – chlorine, other chemicals – but it was also the middle of the night in a small, Midwestern town.

We didn't have a lot of options.

And she was looking sicker by the minute.

I turned back to Baylie, my brow rising desperately. "Her parents were afraid of her coming near water at all, right?"

Baylie nodded.

"Okay, then let's try that."

I jerked my chin toward the bathroom door. Dropping the rag, Baylie hurried toward it while I stood and scooped Chloe into my arms.

She was limp enough to be dead.

Trying to ignore the thought, I started after Baylie.

"You could *kill* her," Ellie begged. "Please, she's the only–"

"Help us or shut up," Baylie snapped from the doorway. Without waiting to see if her words had an effect, she spun back to the bathroom.

Hefting Chloe higher in my arms, I followed her.

The stench of cleaning solution and age filled the tight space, and the fluorescent light overhead buzzed like a demented bee in my ears. Water roared from the tap as Baylie twisted the handle all the way around, and I could hear pipes creaking in the walls. Ignoring all of it, Baylie yanked up on the lever below the faucet, sealing the drain.

Seconds ticked by while the tub began to fill.

"She's our best hope," Ellie said in a small voice.

I glanced back.

Clinging to the side of the door, she remained outside the bathroom, watching us from behind the partial cover of the wall.

"If *any* of the stories are true," she continued as if pleading for us to understand. "We need her to live. We all do."

My brow furrowed.

"Tub's ready," Baylie said behind me.

I pulled my gaze from Ellie and turned to the bathtub. Drawing a breath, I adjusted Chloe in my arms and then bent carefully, lowering her into the water till it covered everything but her head.

Nothing happened.

Air left me. I'd really hoped it'd be that simple. Just water, any water, and she'd be alright.

Not taking her eyes from Chloe, Baylie reached over and turned off the faucet.

The water stilled. Slumped against the side of the tub, Chloe didn't move.

My brow twitched down. She wasn't moving at all. She wasn't even shaking anymore.

A shiver ran over my skin and for a second, I couldn't do anything but stare at her. My heart climbed my throat as carefully, I slid a hand from under her and reached for the side of her neck.

Baylie made a choked noise as she realized what I was doing.

Swallowing hard, I forced myself to feel for her pulse.

A moment crept by.

Her vein quivered beneath my fingertips, so weak I could barely feel it move.

A breath left me.

"I-is she..." Baylie asked tremulously.

"No," I answered. "No, she's–"

Baylie's gasp cut me off.

I looked from her to Chloe and then froze.

A faint, iridescent sheen was creeping along Chloe's legs. There weren't any scales. Nothing of the tail or fin that I'd seen that day she first changed. Just the palest trace of color, dancing in and out of existence like ghostly northern lights inside her skin.

But it was something.

I glanced to Baylie.

She tugged her attention from Chloe to look at me. "Good idea," she breathed.

"You too."

Nodding distantly, she dropped her gaze back to Chloe and the shimmer still twisting through her skin.

I turned to Ellie.

Gripping the side of the door, she was staring at Chloe.

"What did you mean, she's your best hope?" I asked.

She didn't respond.

"Ellie."

The girl blinked, but didn't look at me. "O-old legends. She just..." Ellie exhaled, as though she couldn't believe what she was seeing. "Is she really going to be alright?"

I hesitated. "I don't know."

"Is there anything I can do?"

I glanced back to Baylie, whose face tightened.

A cell phone buzzed in the next room.

I tensed, while Baylie just grimaced at the sound, her reluctance to leave Chloe obvious.

"I'll get that," Ellie offered quickly. She pushed away from the wall and retreated to the motel room.

"Sandra or Chloe's parents?" Baylie commented, as if taking bets on who it'd be.

I didn't answer. I'd figured her parents would've called us thirty seconds after we left. For that matter, I'd figured they would have had the cops and the FBI chasing us by now.

But then, maybe they didn't want the attention. Child and Family Services wouldn't exactly take kindly to their agreement for Chloe to be given drugs and experimented on.

Ellie came back in. She handed the purple-cased cell phone to Baylie, who looked down briefly.

"Chloe's parents win," she muttered.

"Don't answer it," Ellie urged.

Baylie glanced to me. I shook my head.

She clicked the phone to silent and then set it beside the sink.

I returned my attention to Chloe. She seemed to be breathing deeper now. More like she was asleep than a heartbeat from death's door. I rocked back on my heels and looked to Ellie again.

"Legends," I prompted. "Landwalker stories, right?"

Ellie hesitated, something like regret flickering over her face, almost as if she wished she hadn't said anything before. "Yeah." She bit her lip. "Listen, I know you're her friends, but–"

"Tell us," Baylie demanded.

She paused. "Has she said anything to you about it?"

Baylie glanced to me.

"No," I grudged.

Ellie's mouth tightened, and I could see her reluctance becoming determined silence.

"But I'm not sure if she knows any of it either," I persisted. "She's only known she's part dehaian for a few weeks and… and she may not have learned about it when she was away."

"It would help if you told us, though," Baylie pressed.

The girl glanced to Chloe again, considering.

"I know about secrets, Ellie," I risked saying. "About needing to keep them."

Her gaze flicked to me in alarm.

I kept my face as calm as possible, and worked to ignore the way the words made my heart pound. "You can trust us. We're good at secrets." I hesitated. "Please."

Ellie stared at me for a moment, her brow twitching down in time to whatever thoughts were racing behind her eyes. Swallowing hard, she gave a tight nod. "We'll talk when she's awake."

Discomfort still on her face, she pushed away from the door and retreated to the motel room without another word.

Baylie shook her head and made a frustrated noise.

I didn't respond. I could sympathize with wanting to keep things hidden, though in this case, there wasn't a chance in hell I'd let those things stay that way.

But I still got it.

I looked back at Chloe. The shimmering colors on her legs had faded, but her chest continued to rise and fall slowly beneath the water.

Shifting around, I sank onto the cold tile floor, still watching her and ready to wait forever if that was how long it took for her to wake up.

16

CHLOE

The first thing I felt around me was water, and for a moment, I thought we were in the ocean.

Except that the water didn't seem right, and there was a hard surface on my side and back.

Memories started to return.

My heart pounding, I opened my eyes and then winced against the bright light.

I was in a bathtub, in a bathroom I didn't recognize. Water covered me up to my neck and below it, I was still in the blue hospital gown and shorts.

My gaze slid to the side and my brow furrowed at the sight of Baylie and Noah sitting on the floor beside me.

And at the relief in their eyes.

"Hey," Baylie said, blinking and running a hand over her face like she'd just woken up.

I glanced between them warily. "What happened?"

Noah hesitated. "You passed out."

I could hear there was more to it than that in his voice. My gaze flicked to the bathtub and the water covering me. "Passed out," I repeated.

"How do you feel?" Baylie asked.

I wasn't sure how to respond. My body was stiff, like I'd slept in the wrong position for about a year, and the world still seemed shaky, as though it might fly apart if I moved too fast. But the heat in my skin and muscles was gone, and everything didn't hurt like it had.

"How long was I out?" I asked.

Noah paused again. "A while."

My eyes didn't leave him. That wasn't really an answer.

Ellie skidded around the corner of the bathroom, catching herself on the door. "She's awake?"

The girl stared at me, the same relieved look on her face that the others had when I'd opened my eyes. "Are you okay? How're you feeling? Anything hurt or–"

"Ellie," Noah interrupted.

She cut off, breathing hard. Chagrin spread across her face.

I looked between them, a really bad feeling about the time I was unconscious creeping over me.

"You want to try getting up?" Baylie offered before I could ask about it again.

I nodded and pushed away from the side of the tub. My muscles protested, barely able to hold my weight, and Noah reached over quickly, steadying me.

With a grateful, if embarrassed, glance to him, I managed

to reach my feet. Water dripped from the soaked hospital gown and the blue fabric clung to my skin in a way that made a whole other kind of heat start rushing up my neck.

"Let me get you some clothes," Baylie said.

She hurried from the room.

Noah's hands didn't leave my sides.

"Are you alright?" he asked quietly.

I swallowed, my gaze flicking to Ellie. Still holding onto the edge of the door, she watched us. At my glance, she blushed too and then retreated to the other room.

"What happened?" I asked again.

"It doesn't matter."

I looked up at him. His green eyes avoided mine.

"Noah."

"It doesn't," he repeated. "What they tried didn't work, so the rest isn't important. I'm just glad you're awake."

He glanced up to me, and it was my turn to avoid his gaze.

I'd almost forgotten how it felt to have him look at me that way.

"Chloe, about what I–"

Baylie came back in, a bundle of clothes and my shoes in her arms.

Noah grimaced, letting drop whatever he'd planned to say.

"Clear out, eh?" Baylie suggested to him as she set the clothes on the white countertop by the sink.

"Yeah," he agreed.

Not really looking at me, he helped me sit down on the

edge of the tub and then let me go. Without another word, he left the room.

"Here," Baylie said.

Pulling my gaze from him, I tried to focus on what she was offering. We'd been roughly the same size and trading clothes for years, and I paused at the green t-shirt in her hands.

"That's mine," I said.

"No, it's not."

I raised an eyebrow at her and she glanced to the shirt again. "Oh. Well, consider this me giving it back to you then."

My lip twitched. She grinned.

The lightness didn't last long. As quickly as it'd come, her smile flickered and died. Leaving the shirt with me, she went to shut the door.

My hand trembled from the weakness my muscles couldn't seem to overcome as I reached up to untie the string holding the hospital gown closed. With a sharp tug, Baylie yanked a towel from the rack nearby and then handed it to me. While I dried off, she turned away, studying the ground at her feet.

In silence, I changed into the clothes, and Baylie glanced back when I said I was finished. She put her arm around my side, helping me across the room and steadying me on the cold tile.

The others were waiting when we left the bathroom. Sitting on the edge of the bed, Noah watched us, while Ellie stood against the wall, shifting her weight awkwardly and seeming as though she could barely hold back her questions.

I paused, seeing the sunlight slipping past the curtains on the far side of the room. My gaze flicked to the clock on the nightstand, and my heart started to pound again as I spotted the early morning hour.

"Come on," Baylie said.

Noah got up and crossed to the door, leaving the bed to me. As Baylie helped me down, I glanced at him askance.

He was back to not meeting my gaze again.

I hesitated. I wanted to talk to him, I knew we needed to, but there just wasn't time. I'd been unconscious for hours. The whole night, actually.

And Zeke was still out there.

I turned to Ellie. "How do I find Zeke?"

Ellie hesitated, her gaze flicking nervously between the others and me. "Um, look, we really need to talk–"

"Is it about where he is?"

"Well, no..."

"Then we can talk later. I need to find him."

"Don't you think maybe we should call the cops?" Baylie asked. "Tell them what's going on?"

"The cops are in on this," I said. "One of them, anyway. And the others..." I grimaced, Earl's words coming back to me. "Zeke doesn't exist, as far as they're concerned. He doesn't have an ID, family to look for him, anything. These people can just make him disappear."

"But–"

"I can't let him get hurt by this. He's only here because of me."

"But what about *you?*" she pressed. "Chloe, these people could–"

"Where did they take him?" I interrupted, turning to Ellie. I didn't want to hear it. What people could do to me. I'd had more of that than I could handle in the past few weeks and I was doing everything possible to keep from thinking about it now.

Baylie made an angry noise.

"I'm with Baylie," Ellie tried. "I really don't think you–"

"Tell me."

Ellie hesitated, staring at me and looking a bit like she wanted to cry. I felt bad for snapping at her, but there was nothing for it.

I had to find Zeke.

"I-I don't know," Ellie stammered. "I think they probably brought him with you to the lab, since Grandpa got real interested when he heard that there was a full-blood dehaian with you, but he's never told me where to find it. He claimed it wasn't historically relevant yet, so it wasn't important for the database."

"What about those guys he works with? The ones you said took us?"

She shrugged, wincing. "They just come by the house sometimes. I don't think they live around here."

I started to scowl and then paused, a new idea occurring to me. I couldn't force anyone to tell me where this laboratory was – not really, anyway – and asking little Harman was out since the old man would probably just try to hide Zeke the moment he knew someone was looking.

But there was another option.

"Dad went there, though, right?" I asked. "He took Zeke?"

"And picked you up," Ellie agreed, "you know, after…"

I pushed the memory away, covering my discomfort with a quick nod. "Great. Fine." I glanced to Baylie. "Can I borrow your phone?"

She stared at me.

My brow rose at her, anger bubbling up. I needed her help and this was the only option. Why couldn't she see that?

Her head shook. "I'm not–"

"Noah?" I prompted.

His face tightened.

"You can't do this, Chloe!" Baylie protested. "I'm not going to let you just–"

"I have to."

"But you were almost *dead* last night! You can't just go back so they can try it again!"

She turned away, seeming like she was going to cry. By the door, Noah grimaced, dropping his gaze to the ground as though he wished she hadn't said that.

I stared at them. I shouldn't have been shocked, really. I'd seen it on their faces – the fact that something bad had happened. I'd heard it in Noah's voice.

But still… dead?

Trembling, I made myself take a breath. I wasn't, though. I was alive, and the lovely dehaian metabolism that let me go for days without eating or sleeping also meant that right now I felt barely worse than if I'd been getting over a bad cold. So yesterday wasn't important. Near death wasn't important. Saving Zeke was what I needed to focus on.

"I still have to help him," I said, my voice more choked than I would have liked.

Baylie scoffed furiously.

Noah glanced back up at me. "We have to keep you safe too."

I faltered at the look in his eyes.

"Let us get you away from here," he continued. "We can search for Zeke, but you–"

"No."

I hesitated, the word having emerged before I'd really thought it through. But it didn't matter. I couldn't just leave. Just run and hide and hope that somehow, the entire world of monsters didn't find the new place I'd chosen to stay.

It hadn't worked so far.

And that was the point, really. It had never worked. There was always someone else, some*thing* else chasing me. No matter how hard I ran, or how far, another monster was always waiting. I'd run from the Sylphaen and I'd run from Niall. I'd run from Earl and Noah's cousins as well.

At this rate, I'd be running for the rest of my life.

And it still wouldn't help anything at all.

My gaze dropped to the floor, cold settling over me enough to make the hairs on my arms rise. And that was the point too. I'd been scared and I'd wanted safety. I'd wanted to come home, under the belief that here I could pretend none of the horrible past few weeks had happened. But the monsters had followed me home, and the others had just been where I'd left them.

Nothing changed.

So it was time to be done. Done with running and done with trying to hide. For Zeke, for the chance I'd lose him and the possibility this could save his life, it was time to be done.

Baylie made a desperate sound. "Chloe—"

"No!" I snapped.

She blinked.

"I can't risk him dying," I continued, my voice shaking as I tried to soften my tone. "I can't. Even if they don't kill him, the distance from the ocean still could. Full-blood dehaians don't survive for long if they're away from it, and the only reason he made it this far is something to do with..." I kept my gaze from going to Noah, "with being near me. He's here because of *me*, Baylie, and because he wanted to make sure I was safe." I paused. "I can't let him die for that."

Her brow twitched down, and I could still see protests struggling to emerge.

"Please just give me the phone," I begged her.

She exhaled, a pained expression on her face. Shaking her head, she drew the cell from her pocket.

"Thank you."

She didn't respond.

I pressed the button to turn the screen on, and then paused at the sight of the dozens of missed calls.

"They've been trying to reach us all night," Baylie explained quietly.

I hesitated, and then selected the most recent one. The line buzzed while the phone tried to put the call through.

Dad didn't waste any time when he answered.

"Young lady, how *dare* you take my–"

"Dad."

He went quiet for a moment. "Chloe?"

Anger shivered through me and I drew a breath, ordering myself to focus. I would get through this. I'd get the information I needed and then...

Then I'd never come near them again.

The anger grew stronger.

"Yeah," I replied tightly.

"Are you o–"

"I'm alive," I interrupted, biting back the urge to add anything more.

He paused. "Where are you?"

I clenched a hand to the bedspread, crushing it in my fist. "Where did you take Zeke, Dad?"

"That's not–"

"Where is he?" I repeated, my tone harder.

"They're returning him to the ocean. He's fine."

I hesitated. My gaze flicked up to Ellie and quickly, I covered the bottom of the phone. "He says they're taking him back to the ocean."

Ellie's brow furrowed, and after a heartbeat, her head shook as though she couldn't quite believe the possibility.

I lowered my hand from the phone. "Where did you take him before that?"

"Chloe, please, where are you? Your mother and I are—"

I couldn't restrain a furious noise and at it, he cut off.

"I understand if you're confused, honey," he allowed carefully. "Things have changed, but you have to know it's for the best. You're safer this way."

"I'm still dehaian, Dad."

"Chloe… I know this is hard, but you need to—"

"It didn't work. What you and Mom tried to have that man do to me," I shivered, "it didn't work."

He was silent.

I closed my eyes, making myself focus. "I need you to tell me where you took us."

"Zeke won't be there, honey. He—"

"Where?"

Another heartbeat passed. "Let us talk to you. Come meet you. I'll tell you what you want to know, just let us see you first."

By the door, Noah shifted his weight and I looked over to him.

He could hear Dad. I could tell from the expression on his

face. It faltered a bit with embarrassment at my glance, but most of the barely restrained fury remained.

And he was probably right to be angry. I couldn't imagine my parents would make it this easy. Not when yesterday they'd been willing to manipulate me, drug me, and have me experimented on just to get what they wanted.

So this was Dad lying again. Working some plan again.

A quiver ran through me. I wasn't used to thinking about my parents like this. Not quite, anyway. In my head, they'd always sort of been the enemy.

But this was something else.

"Alright," I said.

Noah's brow furrowed in alarm.

"You meet me where you took us."

Dad paused.

"I want to see what was done to me," I pressed. "I want to know what happened."

"Chloe–"

"Or I'm gone. You never see me again. I'm dehaian, Dad. You, your cop friends, and anyone else you send won't stand a chance of staying near the ocean long enough to find me out there."

For a moment, he said nothing.

"Okay," he agreed tightly.

I trembled.

His voice was cold when he continued. "The warehouse outside the Borman Grain plant, fifteen miles south of Midfield on Prairieview Road. I assume that Eleanor girl is still with you. Ask her if you need further directions."

He hung up.

I lowered the phone.

"Chloe, what the hell–"

I tensed, and Noah cut off.

Still shaking, I drew a breath. I knew it wasn't perfect. There wasn't any guarantee that they wouldn't call Harman, that he wouldn't move Zeke. And in any case, we weren't exactly an army. Even if Zeke was there, we couldn't just storm the place.

But it was the best I could do.

"You know where Borman Grain is?" I asked Ellie.

She stared at me.

"Ellie?" I demanded.

Worriedly, she looked to the others. "Uh, yeah. Grandpa's friend owns the place. It's only a few minutes away. But if that's where he–"

"Good. I need to get there."

I pushed away from the bed, and my legs wobbled beneath me. Baylie reached out, catching me.

"This is insane, Chloe," Noah argued. "They're just going to try to get you back again."

I reached my feet. "I know. But what other option is there?"

His mouth tightened and he looked away.

"We could call the police," Baylie suggested incredulously. "Even if Zeke's not in some system, what they're doing still has to be illegal!"

I exhaled. I couldn't stop shivering, like something inside me was just freezing more and more by the second. It felt so strange, so alien and cold, but not remotely like last night, when I'd been sick and scared and aching from what they'd done.

This was something else.

"You can't," Ellie said quietly.

I looked to her and Baylie did the same.

"The chief of police in your town isn't Grandpa's only connection in the legal system. Mom once told me that Grandpa and the... the landwalker elders... they get whatever they want when it comes to the law." She swallowed. "The cops won't do anything if Grandpa's there. No matter what they find."

I stared at her. She gave a tight shrug, looking uncomfortable and embarrassed. "We don't have the same powers as you, so we compensate with, you know, other kinds."

A breath left me. That was it then.

On legs I cursed for being so weak, I started for the door.

"Chloe!"

I looked back. "I'm going, Baylie."

She stared at me. "And you seriously think I'm letting you do that alone?"

At my silence, she scoffed. Shaking her head angrily, she strode toward me.

"Come on," she muttered as she reached over, putting her

arm around my side to steady me. "Let's go find this Zeke guy."

With a dark look to Noah, she nodded toward the door.

He paused, and then sighed. Still grimacing reluctantly, he pulled it open.

Ellie trailed after us as we left the motel room and headed for the car.

⟳ 17 ⟲

ZEKE

I'd lost track of time. The restraints were all that held me up now; my muscles had lost the ability to support me hours ago. More spikes sat immersed in jars on the table – Harman's backups in case he wanted to run further tests – and shivers wracked me from the drugs he'd randomly decided to inject into my veins. Barely clinging to human form, my legs were a mess of iridescent threads tying them together and large bandages where he'd forced my scales to appear and then sheared them off. There wasn't an inch of me that didn't hurt somehow, though at least the ache of the ocean's distance had stopped growing stronger a while ago, even if I didn't know why.

One tiny mercy in this nightmare.

Over the hours, I'd tried using aveluria in my voice – Harman's threats of his friends with cameras be damned – but nothing ever changed. He'd shake his head, give me a tired glare, and then return to his questions with a single-minded intensity that I'd started to see as pure madness. And

240

I couldn't hope to touch him and make the effect of the magic stronger. Any time he came close, he was careful to avoid contact with my skin, except through his tools, needles, and knives.

I thought I'd hated my brothers. Ren for what he was and Niall for what he'd become. I thought I'd hated the Sylphaen for what they wanted to do to Chloe.

I hadn't known what hate was.

"Now, the greliarans say that your people live longer than humans, by maybe fifty years," Harman asked while he held one of the jars up to the light and regarded the contents within. "Is that true?"

I shuddered. I knew what was coming. But I'd be damned if I gave the sick little bastard the satisfaction of thinking he'd broken me.

His mouth tightened with frustration. He reached over, picked up the metal rod on the table, and touched it to my side again.

Electricity shot through my body and I lurched in the restraints.

"I really wish we could get past this," Harman sighed as he returned the rod to the tabletop. "After all, you know I have limited time."

Ragged breaths left me while the shock faded back to a quivering ache. "I... will outlive you," I rasped. "And your children. And theirs."

And in his case, hopefully that outliving would start the

moment I got down from here.

I shivered. I'd never wanted to hurt someone in my life as much as I wanted to hurt the old man at that table.

"Interesting." He turned back to his notebook and scribbled something down. "By *how* long exactly?"

I tugged at the restraints, not answering. The locks holding the bars on my wrists and legs had to break soon. It'd been hours and they'd never budged, but by all that was holy, if I could just get the right leverage and angle, they had to break soon. Daylight was pouring through the grimy windows high on the metal walls, and I couldn't hope those greliarans would wait too much longer before demanding their chance at me.

He exhaled tiredly. "This really–"

The door on the opposite side of the room opened as if in answer to my thoughts. My heart climbed my throat as Harman scrambled to his feet.

"I'm sorry, sir," came a familiar voice. "I tried to tell them you weren't done."

My brow drew down at the sight of the scrawny police officer from Reidsburg. Aaron, I thought the chief had called him. His baggy uniform had been replaced with a lab coat, which fit no better than the uniform had, and his gaze darted to me as though he expected me to burst from the restraints at any moment.

Which would have been great, really. I would have loved to oblige.

Richard shoved past him.

"You asked for hours," he snapped to Harman. "You've had hours." He scanned me over. "And you haven't exactly left us much to enjoy killing."

His sons came into the room after him, leaving Aaron standing by the door and fidgeting like a nervous bird. Their burning eyes locked on me as they fanned out, moving like they were circling their prey while cracks spread through their skin.

My hands pulled harder at the restraints.

"I still have questions!" Harman protested. "You can't take him yet."

Richard ignored him. Coming up to me, he paused. "What do you think, boys? One leg broken? Maybe some ribs? How much of a chase do we want?"

Harman made a desperate sound, looking between them all while his hands clutched at the underside of the table. "You *can't*," he insisted. "I haven't even gotten to my tests of our new suppression drug, and we—"

"Break both," Wyatt growled.

"I'm *warning* you!" Harman cried. "Give me a bit more time!"

Richard chuckled. He pulled back a fist as fissures ran through his skin and hunger swallowed everything human in his eyes.

I tensed.

Wyatt made an angry sound and Richard froze. His attention snapped toward the far wall as his sons' did the same.

A growl left Richard, the sound building until it turned into a roar. His fist swung forward, slamming into the metal sheet behind me and propelling it backward. I flew with it, crashing to the concrete with a force that sent pain throbbing through every bone in my body.

I twisted, trying to get a glimpse of the greliarans, and then froze.

The bars across my left wrist and my feet had both moved.

Barely breathing, I looked to the other side of the room.

"What is it?" Harman asked, trying to keep an eye to me and the others at the same time. "What's going on?"

Snarling curses, Richard didn't respond. He closed his eyes briefly and then glanced to his sons.

"Earl?" one of them asked.

"He got arrested, moron," another retorted.

"Noah," Wyatt growled.

I stopped breathing entirely. If he was here, then Chloe…

"Take the front," Richard snapped to Wyatt. "Owen, Clay, use the back door and get around the sides. Brock, you're with me. We're guarding the scum-sucker." He paused, looking to the wall as though he could see through it. "And you three? You get your hands on Noah, you break things till he stops moving but you keep him alive."

"What if his scale-skin girlfriend's with him?" Wyatt asked.

Richard gave him a dry look.

Wyatt smiled. Motioning to two of his brothers, he strode from the room. The remaining guy headed for something behind me. I craned my neck around and watched him take up position by a steel door I hadn't realized was there.

"N-now," Harman stammered. "If that young lady's here, you need to understand, she won't be a dehaian anymore. And I need her for further treatments and testing, so–"

"We agreed to let her go," Richard said. "We didn't say anything about what we'd do if she came back looking for us."

"There's no guarantee she's looking for–"

"She's probably searching for him. We're here." Richard grinned, the expression like ice. "That's close enough." He returned his attention to the wall. "Now shut it. They just drove up."

Harman fidgeted with the table, his eyes going from me to the others and back.

I drew a careful breath as silence settled over the room. I needed to move fast if I was going to get out of all these restraints before the greliarans could stop me.

Before they could kill me. Or her.

I swallowed. The guy behind me was smaller, though the distinction was only relative to his brothers, and maybe that would give me a chance. But Richard was still here, my legs were a mess, I'd been immobilized for hours, and only that little bastard knew what drugs he'd given me in that time.

A shiver ran through me. I needed the right moment. A distraction to give me long enough to just get to my feet.

And if Chloe really was out there, I needed it to come damn soon.

18

CHLOE

"Listen," Ellie tried. "When we get there… maybe you could just stay in the car? Let me go in and see if Zeke is there? We don't even have to stay around for your parents. It's going to take them longer to get here than us anyway."

I glanced to her. On the seat beside me, she fidgeted, casting worried looks from me to the country road and back.

Seeing my expression, she winced. "I-I know. It's just… Grandpa could hurt you. He's not a bad man, but if he got his hands on you again, or your parents came and tried to… I just don't…"

Her gaze flicked to Baylie and Noah up front. She went silent, her worried expression deepening.

From the corner of my eye, I watched her, trying not to be creeped out. I didn't know what to make of the girl. Pretty like a doll and anxious as a rabbit in a dog house, Ellie seemed to be a bundle of things she couldn't quite bring herself to say. She'd saved my life. I knew that. And she'd gotten me away from my parents and her own grandfather. I was grateful as anything for that too.

But I barely knew her. I'd met her less than five minutes before Harman jabbed me with a needle – another needle; I was really sick of needles – and prior to that, I'd never seen her before in my life. I supposed anyone could try to save somebody they'd just met from something they thought was wrong, but still… it felt odd.

And somehow disturbing.

It was mostly the way she looked at me. Like she knew me, or something about me. I hadn't forgotten how she'd wanted to talk earlier – hopefully about that, whatever *that* was – but meanwhile, it was just weird having someone look at you the way she was looking at me.

Shifting around on the seat, I forced my attention to the fields. There wasn't really time to talk about it now, though. I needed to figure out how I was going to get Harman to let Zeke go, assuming the old man was at this Borman Grain place. And if he wasn't, I needed to figure out what I'd do then.

I hadn't come up with anything so far.

Baylie steered the car past a curve, and beyond the turn, there was just more empty country road. I tried not to sigh. Small rises in the terrain and the general height of the corn made it hard to see the horizon, but the place my dad said he'd taken us had to be around here somewhere. I had to believe Ellie wouldn't have sent us in the wrong direction;

she'd done nothing but help us thus far. But the drive felt like it was taking forever.

Another curve followed, and then a third. I shifted on the seat again, debating whether to question Ellie about her directions.

And then a collection of grain silos came into view.

"There," Ellie said quietly.

I didn't take my eyes from the tall structures. Maybe three miles away, they appeared and disappeared over the tops of the corn.

Noah tensed, a curse escaping him. "Pull over," he ordered Baylie.

Glancing to him in alarm, she steered the car to the side of the road.

"What?" I asked. "What is it?"

He closed his eyes briefly and then looked back. His gaze flicked from me to Ellie, and I saw frustration flash across his face.

"They're here," he admitted grudgingly.

I paused in confusion. And then it clicked.

"Wait," I said, my heart tripping over itself as it started to race. "You mean, your–"

"All five of them. They know I'm here too. Second I picked up on them, they did the same, and now they're hiding."

I stared at him, fighting not to give into the panic bubbling up inside. Zeke had to be there too, then. If Noah's family was at the warehouse, then he had to be as well, but...

Zeke was fine. He wasn't dead. They wouldn't still be there if he was dead.

"You need to get out of here," Noah said to me.

"No, I'm not—"

"You have to. They'll—"

"I'm not leaving him!"

Noah stopped. Awkward silence fell on air still ringing from my shout. His brow twitched down and I couldn't read the look in his eyes.

"Okay," he agreed, his voice quiet and tight.

A breath left me.

He paused for a heartbeat, still watching me with that strange look in his eyes, and then he shifted back around on the seat. "Get us a bit closer," he said to Baylie in the same tone. "I need to see where they're hiding."

She put the car back in gear. In silence, we drove down the country highway and turned onto the road leading to the silos.

The cornfields fell away and more of the complex appeared. A long road stretched from the main highway to Borman Grain, which mostly seemed to consist of a cluster of square buildings next to the towering silos. Those, in turn, were surrounded on two sides by large, white storage domes that looked like they were preparing to take off at the command of the mothership. An aluminum-sided warehouse waited closer to the road, while a train track for shipments ran nearby.

"Stop here," Noah ordered.

Baylie did.

I swallowed hard, studying the warehouse. Maybe half the length of a football field, and a quarter the width, the warehouse sat to the left of the road and far from the silos. Enormous garage doors, all of them closed, formed the longest side, with a single, human-sized door near the corner. A narrow, gravel parking lot fronted the building and held a brown Buick and a maroon SUV.

Ellie made a worried noise. "Grandpa."

Noah pulled his gaze from the building. Reaching to the middle of the dashboard, he flipped the air conditioning to full blast, and then switched on the radio as well. As the white-noise drone filled the car, he turned to look at me.

I tensed, silently daring him to try to make me stay here.

He seemed to see it. His jaw muscles jumped.

"Can you run?" he asked.

I nodded, and attempted to ignore the worried look Baylie gave me in response.

He echoed the motion. "Then stay behind me. Walk on the grass not the gravel; they'll have a harder time hearing that. And–"

"You're greliaran, aren't you?"

He blinked and turned to Ellie.

"That's why you know about secrets," she said. "You–"

She cut off, her brow furrowing, and she looked between us as though she couldn't figure out what she was seeing.

"Listen," he continued to me, his gaze flicking to Ellie distractedly. "They're going to come after you. I can't stop all of them. But when that happens…" He grimaced, as if he hated the words. "You run. We're stronger, but you're faster. So just run like hell."

"What about Zeke?"

"I'll—"

"I can get him," Ellie interrupted.

Noah glanced to her again.

"You distract them," she said. "I'll get him."

"They'll kill you," Noah argued.

She shook her head. "Grandpa will stop them. If he's in there, he'll stop them."

"He'll stop you too," I protested.

"I can get Zeke," she insisted.

I stared at her. I hardly knew her, and she wanted me to trust her with Zeke's life? Sure, she'd helped me, but when it came to him…

There wasn't a choice. We were running out of time.

"Fine," I managed. "Just be careful."

Ellie nodded.

"Stay here," Noah said to Baylie. "Watch for us and, if Chloe's parents show up, do your best to keep them out of the way. We'll be back as soon as possible and we'll need to leave fast."

She grimaced, but made a grudging noise of agreement.

He glanced to me. "Run. Try to lose them in the fields if you can. And then circle back. We should have Zeke by then, so come meet us at the car and we'll get out of here. Alright?"

I swallowed. It sounded a lot like a best-case scenario. I just hoped it worked. "Yeah."

He climbed from the car. I followed, my legs quivering unsteadily for a moment before consenting to hold me.

We started toward the warehouse. Wind carried over the fields around us, along with a beeping noise from a distant semi reversing near the silos. Several dozen cars filled the parking lots next to the square buildings of the main complex, and as we walked over the crabgrass and dirt, a train rumbled along the track, heading for the silos as well.

The place wasn't abandoned or isolated by any stretch of the imagination. It seemed a strange location for a secret lab.

But that could turn out to be a good thing. Maybe, if Noah's family tried to come after us, the fact there were others around would keep them from killing anyone.

My stomach turning flip-flops, I kept pace with Noah. Ellie stayed near me, radiating nervous energy and trying to look in every direction at once.

We drew closer to the warehouse.

The door creaked as it swung ponderously open. I stopped and Noah did too. With a tiny whimper, Ellie froze.

No one came out. Nothing moved.

I glanced to Noah.

"Bait," he mouthed.

I nodded.

Heart pounding, I scanned the fields. There wasn't anything to do. We had to keep going.

Trembling with adrenaline, I followed him toward the door. My skin shivered with the desire to let my spikes grow and the world sharpened as my eyes changed of their own accord. I could see hairline fissures slipping along Noah's arms, appearing like threads of lightning and then vanishing almost as quickly, while a red glow flecked the green of his eyes.

A burly young man stepped outside. Well above six feet tall, with the build of a football player on every steroid known to God or man, he smirked at us as he crossed his arms, making his biceps bulge.

"Hey there, cuz," he drawled.

Noah ignored him, checking the area quickly.

"What? No hello? Thought you'd want to finally introduce me to your little friend."

The guy's gaze went to me, and his eyes grated down me like he could see straight through my clothes.

I tensed, pulling back involuntarily.

A snarl twitched his face, buried so fast it looked like a muscle spasm, and a shiver ran through him. "Name's Wyatt," he managed, a growl coming into his voice. "Been looking forward to getting my hands on you, pretty."

Footsteps crunched on the gravel of the parking lot.

Two more guys, obviously his brothers, emerged from either side of the warehouse.

"Chloe," Noah said carefully.

I glanced to him.

Noah didn't look away from his cousins. Cracks spread

through his arms and face, unrestrained now, and his eyes went red. "Run."

He lunged at Wyatt.

I spun and took off.

The nearest cousin shouted and scrambled after me, his hands swiping the air as I passed. Adrenaline flooded me, prickling through my skin and setting my heart racing. The gravel parking lot fell away, and then the road. Grass flashed by beneath my feet while in my ears, the wind rushed like the ocean.

I threw a look over my shoulder.

They were still coming. I couldn't see Ellie anywhere. Noah was struggling with Wyatt, but as I watched, Wyatt shoved him hard to the side, trying to break Noah's hold to join the chase.

And the others were gaining.

Fighting for more speed, I ran for the silos.

19

ZEKE

Voices carried from beyond the walls of the warehouse, and I strained to hear if Chloe was among them. On the other side of the room, Richard stood motionless by the door while Harman fidgeted next to the long, steel table. Behind me, Brock twitched as he fought to stay still, his eyes already glowing and fissures permeating his skin.

Someone outside shouted.

Richard swore. "Stay here!" he snapped at Brock as he ripped open the door.

He raced from the room.

I looked from Brock to Harman, and then yanked at the restraints.

The one on my left wrist gave enough to let my hand slip by, while the bar on my feet popped free of the table entirely. Rolling to the side, I shoved hard at the metal holding my other wrist.

Brock made a furious noise. His footsteps thudded toward

me.

Something beneath the table snapped. The restraint gave away.

I scrambled aside just as his fist slammed down where I'd been.

"You scale-skin bastard," Brock growled. "Get back here."

Casting quick glances from him to Harman, I retreated as my few remaining spikes emerged to stand out on my arms. Adrenaline couldn't fully drown the burning pain in my muscles, or stop the way my body was shaking. My legs were so wobbly, they felt like they'd change at any moment, becoming a tail that'd get me killed.

Brock stalked toward me, his face a tangle of glowing cracks extending from eyes that were nothing but impossibly red fire.

"I am going to *gut* you," he snarled, "you disgusting little–"

He charged.

I tumbled to the side, narrowly avoiding stabbing myself with my spikes as I hit the floor. Skidding on the concrete, Brock spun and then lunged at me again.

Frantic, I rolled and scrambled for my feet.

His hands caught my back and shoved me. Harman stumbled away with a panicked shout as I crashed to the ground only inches from the table and his research. Ignoring him, I rolled again, trying to spot Brock before he could grab me.

My gaze caught on the underside of the table and suddenly, I realized what Harman had been holding onto this entire time.

A gun.

An enormous, double-barreled shotgun.

Lunging up, I snagged the weapon and ripped it from the straps holding it to the table. Brock's red eyes went wide at the sight, and with a roar, he rushed at me again.

I swung the gun around, notched it to my shoulder fast as I could, and then pulled the trigger.

The recoil nearly took my arm off.

Brock stopped a few feet from me, alarm spreading across his face. My ears rang from the blast, but I didn't look away from him as he stumbled.

His fiery eyes blinked. Dark blood spread across the chest of his tight t-shirt.

He crumpled to his knees and then toppled sideways to the ground.

Shaking, I clutched the edge of the table and tugged myself upright on legs that still felt like they wanted to change.

Harman stood motionless, staring at me with his arms frozen in mid-reach for the jars and papers still scattered on the table.

A shiver ran through me. My grip tightened on the gun.

The door on the far side of the room burst open. Harman's granddaughter raced in.

She skidded to a stop, her eyes going wide at the sight of me and the shotgun.

"E-Ellie, what are you–" Harman stammered. "Get out of here, girl! He'll–"

"Please," she interrupted him, lifting her hands as if to show she had no weapons. Her gaze darted from my legs to the jars on the tabletop, and she swallowed hard. "Please, I-I'm sorry. Please hear me. I'm so sorry for what he did."

My brow drew down.

"Please don't shoot him," she begged.

"Ellie, get out of here," Harman urged.

My hand twitched on the gun.

"Please!" Ellie cried. She took a breath and inched a step closer. "Please, Zeke. It's Zeke, right? Just… please. I'm here to help. I don't want to hurt you. I'm only here to help."

She came another step into the room.

"Don't let him near you, girl!" Harman cried. "They just need to touch you and then you'll be–"

"Grandpa, shut up!" she shouted, not looking away from me. A choked noise escaped her. "Just… shut up." She swallowed hard again. "Zeke, Chloe's out there. The greliarans are going after her and that…" her gaze flicked to the gun, "that could stop them."

"Where?" I demanded.

She nodded toward the door behind her. "This way."

I glanced to Harman, trembling. I didn't know what I wanted to do to him. Something. Anything.

So much I didn't know where to begin.

"*Please*," Ellie implored.

My gaze twitched back to her. Letting out an unsteady breath, I headed for the door.

Harman made a panicked sound. "Eleanor, get back! You don't—"

"How *could* you, Grandpa? *How?*"

She retreated hastily as I came near, terror flashing through her light brown eyes, though the expression turned to pain again when she looked back to her grandfather.

I ignored it all. My hand gripping the gun and my body still trembling with the urge to use it, I walked out of the room.

∽ 20 ∽

NOAH

I heard Chloe take off to my right while Ellie bolted for the side of the warehouse to my left, and despite everything, I was grateful. These damn greliaran instincts were screaming for me to kill everything in reach, and the girls were a distraction I didn't need right now.

Because if a gorilla ever existed in quasi-human form, it was my cousin.

My hands gripped Wyatt's shoulders and my feet dug into the gravel as I tried to drive him backward. He twisted in my grasp, attempting to use my own force to throw me. I shifted my balance to stay upright, and then adjusted a second time as he tried again.

He snarled. Chloe was getting farther away. He wanted to join the chase.

Something slammed into me from the side. I hit the gravel and rolled, coming back up fast and looking around for whatever had just barreled into me.

Uncle Richard stood where we'd been. Flecks of red light glowed in his eyes. Cracks no wider than pencil lead twisted along his arms.

And that was it. He'd knocked me down, and he'd barely even changed yet.

I made myself keep breathing. Against Wyatt, I'd stood a chance.

Richard was another story entirely.

"Wyatt, go," Richard ordered.

His son scrambled to his feet and took off after Chloe. Richard twitched to the side, blocking me when I moved to follow.

Heart pounding, I stopped, my gaze flicking from him to my cousins and back.

"You really want to do this, Noah?" he threatened. "My boys are going to tear that girl apart either way."

A growl slipped from me.

His lip curled as his skin changed. I tensed, knowing what was coming.

He charged.

I braced myself as his shoulder hit me like a battering ram, driving me backward to the ground. Twisting, I avoided his fist as it slammed down where my head had been. I punched at him, succeeding in knocking his head to the side.

But nothing more.

He snarled.

His fist landed hard. Stars scattered across my vision. I

swung again blindly, hitting his midsection, though it made less difference than if I'd hit a wall.

"Disgrace," Richard spat. "You're just a fucking–"

A gunshot inside the warehouse cut him off.

He shoved away from me. Rolling to the side, I coughed and spit blood onto the gravel.

My ears were ringing, but I could just make out the sound of Ellie's voice, though her actual words were a garble over the noise in my head. Richard heard her though. I could tell from the rage on his face.

I thought he'd looked mad at me.

I'd never seen anything like his expression now.

He took off around the corner of the warehouse, and the door that must have been beyond it.

I shoved up from the gravel and went after him.

He heard me coming, and before I could reach him, he spun, grabbing after me. Ducking fast, I evaded his grasp and then punched hard at his side. He tensed, taking the blow, and his fist came back like a jackhammer into my ribs.

I stumbled.

With a furious noise, he thrust me aside and turned for the warehouse again.

And then he froze.

I looked over.

Several yards away, Zeke stood, his eyes on Richard and a shotgun in his hands. Large bandages dotted his legs randomly and burns scarred his sides, and even from this distance I could see him shaking. Ellie hovered a few feet from his back, her gaze darting between us and Zeke as if she couldn't figure out which of us to stay farther away from.

A low growl built in Richard's chest.

Zeke aimed the gun at my uncle. "Back off," he ordered.

"Where's my *son?*" Richard snarled, the words barely human.

Zeke inched in the direction of Baylie's car, keeping the gun level. Ellie hurried to stay behind him. "You heard me."

Richard's growl got louder. Zeke tightened his grip on the gun.

Police sirens carried over the fields, the sound so faint Zeke and Ellie gave no sign of noticing. But I could tell Richard heard. His head twitched to the left, toward the noise, and the growl cut off.

Zeke's brow drew down cautiously.

I hesitated. Baylie shouldn't have called the cops. She knew it wouldn't help anything. But perhaps someone at the grain company had heard the gunshot over the distance. Or Ellie's grandfather had called in his allies.

Neither option was good. The police would be a serious problem, because chances were that Brock was dead in there, given the size of the gun Zeke was holding and the fact my cousin hadn't left the warehouse this entire time. At close enough range, a cannon like that would do serious damage, even with our defenses. It was hard to feel sorry. I knew I probably should, since Brock was technically family and all. But that knowledge didn't make the feeling come.

And didn't change the fact cops would mean all of us getting arrested and Chloe ending up squarely back in her parents' hands.

I looked to Ellie, catching her eye. I tilted my head toward the car with an urgent expression.

Swallowing hard, she inched to the other side of Zeke and started for the vehicle, keeping her attention on my uncle. Without lowering the weapon, Zeke followed.

Richard shuddered, clearly torn between pursuing them and continuing toward the warehouse.

I moved cautiously after Ellie, and saw Richard's head twitch again when he heard my feet on the gravel. Watching me from the corner of his eye, he gave another low snarl.

Backpedaling, Ellie put more distance between herself and him even as Zeke did the same.

Richard strode for the warehouse door.

Ellie ran as Baylie began driving toward us. Keeping the gun pointed toward Richard's back, Zeke followed at a hobbling walk.

And that wasn't fast enough. Not if the cops were coming. Not in the time it would take Richard to confirm that the dehaian had just killed his son.

The dehaian Chloe loved.

I shivered, watching him, and then drew a rough breath, driving away the instincts and the darker things I didn't want to think about as I forced my skin to change to human again.

"Run," I told him, a growl still lurking in my voice.

His face tightened. He kept retreating at the same pace.

"Damn you, run."

"Can't."

His gaze flicked to me, all dark and challenging and really making me want to punch him just for existing. Fighting hard against the impulse, I glanced to his legs and the silver threads hanging there as though they'd grown from his skin.

The growl grew stronger. I shook my head, turning the sound to a curse. "Come on," I snapped.

I strode over and snagged his arm, throwing it around my shoulder.

"Where's Chloe?" Zeke demanded, his words coming in short gasps while he attempted to keep pace at my side.

"On her way," I replied, hoping it was true.

A roar sounded from inside the warehouse.

My heart climbed my throat. Zeke grunted, adjusting his other hand on the gun as he tried to move faster.

Baylie pulled her car up in front of us. Ellie tugged open the rear door before retreating quickly to the opposite side of the vehicle.

I barely kept myself from throwing Zeke in. Gripping the top of the car, he managed to climb inside while I hurried for the other door.

Richard raced from the warehouse.

I swung into the passenger seat.

"Chloe?" Baylie cried.

"We'll find her. Go!"

She hit the gas. Gravel spewed from beneath the tires as she whipped the car through a tight turn and then sped back toward the road.

$\curvearrowright$ 21 $\curvearrowleft$

CHLOE

I'd never run this fast in my life.

And Noah's cousins were closing in behind me.

Concrete turned to gravel beneath my shoes as I left the parking lot and raced toward the silos. Tall as skyscrapers, the towers blocked the midmorning sun. Shadows swallowed me as I darted between the buildings, while a few dozen feet away, a group of workers looked over in alarm to see me shoot past.

I ignored them, glancing back. The cousins were still gaining. And to make matters worse, Wyatt had joined the chase. In the distance, Noah was struggling with a man so large, he could only be his uncle.

And neither Ellie nor Zeke were anywhere to be seen.

Sunlight glared in my eyes as I raced out from between the rows of silos. Ahead, empty fields and distant farmhouses waited, none of them promising a single hope for escape from the monsters snarling behind me.

I veered right, running alongside the towers as fast as I

could. I heard the cousins shout when they emerged from the rows as well.

Gasping, I fought for more speed. I couldn't keep this pace up for much longer. However fast Noah thought dehaians could run, it meant nothing compared to the aftereffects of what Harman had done to me.

Aftereffects which were going to get me killed if something didn't change soon.

In my side, a muscle began to cramp as if in answer to the thought, sending stabbing sensations through me with every breath. My other muscles had long since started protesting with throbbing aches of their own and my lungs burned despite the cool morning air. Pained noises escaped me, sounding nearly like sobs to my ears. Gritting my teeth against it all, I threw a glance over my shoulder.

One of them reached out to grab me and pull me down.

I choked, my feet stopping of their own accord and I ducked fast to the right. His hand swiped the air, missing me by inches. He stumbled, overbalanced by the effort, but then his brother was there. I darted to the side and felt his fingers brush my arm, closing a heartbeat too slowly to grab me but burning hot like coals when they touched my skin. I gasped, twisting away, and then I was running along the rows of silos again, leaving the greliarans snarling furiously at my back.

Noah and Ellie had to have gotten Zeke out of there by now. It'd been an eternity, or maybe just a minute, but surely they'd gotten Zeke out.

The collection of silos felt like it would never end.

I bolted past the final tower and then looked to the warehouse, hoping to see Zeke so I could circle back and get out of here too.

My breath caught. Baylie's car was racing away.

Terrified confusion hit me, making my steps falter. They were leaving? Why were they leaving?

A man ran from the warehouse, chasing them as they sped off. A dozen yards ahead of him and gaining distance with every heartbeat, the car skidded onto the road and headed left.

My gaze went from the car to the country highway running parallel with the grain company property. She'd turn onto it. That was where Baylie was going. And since it was directly in my path, I could meet her there, get in the car, and get the hell out of this place.

I hoped.

Gasping down another painful breath, I forced myself to run faster. Gravel became scrub grass under my feet, hiding sinkholes and rocks that threatened to trip me. Everything in me wanted to stop, if only to make my muscles quit hurting with each motion.

The car veered onto the road ahead.

I looked back. The first two guys had slowed, their expressions like they'd used up all the speed they had in trying to reach me that first time.

But Wyatt was still there. And he was gaining.

Desperately, I fought to keep running. The wind whistled

in my ears and my gaze was locked on Baylie's car.

She pulled to a screeching stop thirty yards ahead and I could see her twist in the driver's seat to yell at someone behind her. People moved in the shadows of the vehicle, and then someone scrambled from the passenger side door.

Noah.

With a shotgun in his hands.

"Chloe, move!" he shouted.

I ducked to the side.

The gun went off.

Behind me, Wyatt cried out. I couldn't tell if the sound was more fury or pain, and I didn't bother to check. The last of the field passed beneath me, and then the ditch at the side of the road as well. The rear car door opened as I scrambled up the slope and Zeke reached out to me from inside.

I choked, relief overwhelming the pain. He was alright. He was here.

His hand caught mine. With a grimace, he tugged me into the car and then caught me, his arm wrapping around my shoulders as if to hold me there.

Baylie smashed the gas pedal to the floor.

Gravity pushed me back in the seat and shoved the car door closed at my side.

"Are you okay?" Zeke asked.

I nodded. My heart was still racing and my muscles ached, but nothing mattered quite as much as him being there. Being okay.

My gaze registered the bandages on his legs. The burn marks on his sides. The way his body was shaking. I pushed away from him, my breath catching at the fear that touching him might hurt him more.

Baylie made a panicked noise. I looked back. Wyatt was still struggling after us, blood on his arm and his face a twisted mess of rage. The other cousins remained by the silos, not bothering to try catching up since there was no chance of that now.

And by the warehouse, my parents' sedan was pulling into the drive. Cop cars raced toward the grain factory from the other direction, their lights flashing in colors that felt too bright even over the distance. Harman was rushing from the warehouse door, his arms waving toward the police and a few other figures I didn't recognize following on his heels.

But Harman didn't look toward us. And the large guy who'd been chasing Baylie's car was nowhere to be seen.

The road dipped down a small incline and the terrain swallowed my view.

I turned back. In the front seat, Noah was watching me, while Baylie kept casting glances in the rearview mirror to me and the road.

"Everybody else alright?" I asked breathlessly.

Noah nodded and Baylie did the same. I glanced to Zeke, my eyebrows rising questioningly, while on the other side of him, Ellie seemed to be trying to keep as close to the opposite door as possible.

Zeke's arm tightened around my shoulders, bringing me back to his side. I saw Noah drop his gaze away, his jaw muscles jumping.

Discomfort moved through me. Uncertain what to do or how to feel past the gratitude that we had all escaped from there, I looked away from Zeke and watched the silos disappear over the horizon.

It didn't take Baylie long to want to pull over, and when we reached a small forest preserve with empty picnic tables near the road, that was exactly what she did.

She turned around in the seat to look at me. "So now—"

Ellie scrambled from the car, cutting off her words. Brow furrowing, Baylie stared after her.

"What?" she called.

The girl didn't respond, but Zeke sighed. My brow drawing down in an expression that probably wasn't far from Baylie's, I glanced to him. Ellie had been plastered to the other door for every minute we'd been driving, and spent most of that time eyeing Zeke.

Not explaining, Zeke nudged my shoulder. We climbed from the car, while in the front seats, Baylie and Noah did the same.

"*What?*" Baylie repeated to Ellie, closing her door.

"I'm not going to hurt you," Zeke said with exasperation

as he leaned on the car for support.

Confused, I looked between them.

"We don't have to just touch you," he continued in the same tone. "We have to want to do that, and *trust* me, I don't."

The caution didn't leave her eyes, even as my confusion cleared.

"What're we talking about here?" Baylie asked.

Ellie's face took on a warning look. "You need to stay away from him. If he touches you, then–"

"That's not true," I interrupted hurriedly. Baylie didn't need more reasons to be freaked out about dehaians. "That whole thing. It's just landwalker crap."

Ellie blinked.

"We have to *want* to," Zeke said to her again, speaking each word slowly.

"But you can."

I turned to Noah in surprise. He didn't look away from Zeke.

"If you *want* to," Noah continued. "You take away people's free will. Get them to do whatever you want. You kill them by making them unable to be away from you."

Zeke paused, watching Noah.

"It's illegal, though," I insisted into the silence. "And murder."

Noah didn't respond.

"The greliarans say it's true," Ellie pressed.

I looked back to her.

"Oh yeah," Zeke commented coldly. "Turns out the land-walkers have been working with the greliarans. And not just her grandfather; that scrawny cop from Reidsburg was at the warehouse too."

Ellie dropped her gaze away.

I glanced between her and Noah, alarmed. "Is that true?"

Ellie didn't respond.

"That's why his family was there," Zeke said, jerking his chin toward Noah. "Her grandfather made a deal with them. They stay away from you, they get to kill me." His face tightened with anger. "After he was done experimenting, that is. Seems that's been the landwalker and greliaran deal for years."

I swallowed.

"Not with all of us," Noah said. "I've never heard of that."

Zeke didn't say anything, but at his expression, Noah's face darkened.

I drew a breath. I wanted to know more about this deal between the greliarans and landwalkers, in the way people had of wanting to know more about the terrifying thing so they could decide just how much they should be panicking. But there wasn't time. Everything else aside, my parents could still be chasing us, or sending the cops to do the same. We had to figure out what to do next, and the last thing we needed was to fight among ourselves.

"Okay, listen," I said to Ellie. "I don't care what the greliarans said. Nothing will happen to you if you touch us. It has to be intentional and no one here is going to do it anyway. So please, calm down."

Her face took on a defensive cast.

"You wanted to talk to me about something," I pressed on. "Was it about that?"

She shook her head.

"The greliarans?" I prompted.

Ellie swallowed. "No, it's…" She glanced to the others. "Look, could we maybe, um…"

My brow drew down as I followed her gaze to Noah, Zeke, and Baylie. I could tell what she was asking, and the creeped out feeling I'd had around her earlier started to return.

"You can talk in front of them," I told her.

Her mouth tightened.

"Ellie," Noah tried. "What the hell is it already?"

The girl hesitated. "Alright," she agreed reluctantly, looking back at me. "It's… it's about you. And it's kind of… big."

The disturbed feeling grew. "What about me?"

Her brow furrowed, as though she was searching for the right words. "Well, um, you know about landwalkers and dehaians, right? How we used to be the same?"

I nodded.

"There's a reason we're not anymore. And that reason has a lot to do with something called the Beast."

I tensed.

"You've heard of it?" she asked, reading something in my expression.

"I've heard it mentioned, yeah," I allowed, stopping myself from glancing to Zeke. His brother had brought it up after he'd kidnapped me, as had the Sylphaen pretending to be EMTs back at the cabin.

They'd all said it was coming, and they'd made it sound like it had something to do with me.

"Well, the history is tangled up in a lot of different versions but... it sort of goes like this. The Beast was a force, created by dehaians a long time ago. Back then, dehaians could live on land or in the sea without any trouble, because they had a relationship with the magic in the ocean that I guess you could call synergistic. The dehaians used magic to survive beneath the water, they sustained themselves on it when they couldn't sleep or eat, and they carried it with them when they went on land. In turn, the ocean's magic was really strong. It was almost like a life force all on its own, strengthened by the exchange of energy from the dehaians leaving the sea for deep inland and then returning again.

"Some of our ancestors, though, they didn't want to just live in the ocean. They could survive inland, as well as beneath the water, so they tried to expand their territory. A lot of their people already lived on land, especially on these certain islands out in the Pacific. So they figured they should just establish themselves there formally. But the humans who lived on the nearby islands, they didn't like that. They thought those places were theirs. And they were involved in using the ocean's magic too, and didn't like the competition."

Noah grimaced. "The ones who made us," he said, only partly asking.

Ellie nodded uncomfortably. "There was a war. The dehaians fought against the humans, and they were winning, but then those humans who'd studied magic... they made weapons. The greliarans. So then the dehaians made a weapon too and theirs... well, theirs didn't start out human. They used the magic of the ocean. They contained it somehow. Controlled it in a way no one ever had before. I mean, hundreds of dehaians, all working together to create one thing with a common purpose... nobody had done that. But it formed this... thing. A force of magic that was almost *alive*. That they could control, and that was tied to their magic like a dog on a leash. And they could turn it on anyone they chose.

"The stories say it was terrible. Like a hurricane with a mind, but one that could shake the ground, exist above the water or below it with equal ease, and strike at any target just as its masters ordered. But the thing was... it was ocean magic. It existed as a part of that synergy. And after it destroyed the islands, tearing them apart and dragging them down into the ocean and drowning just... just *everyone* there..." She exhaled. "It turned on the dehaians. Maybe it needed more magic. Maybe it didn't like being controlled. I don't know. But it did, and it just drained the magic right out of them. Dehaians don't survive without that. They're not like humans. They need magic to live. And with that thing coming after them..."

She shook her head. "They ran. They tried to hide. And

when nothing worked, when the Beast kept hunting them down and draining them and never growing weaker no matter how far inland they stayed… they came up with another solution. They'd use their magic to change what they were. To transform their own magical and physical selves so that what the Beast fed on from them wouldn't exist anymore. They split their own characteristics, abilities, *everything*, and made what we have now: dehaians who can't leave the ocean and landwalkers who can't come near the sea. It worked, too. The Beast never went after the landwalkers and it ignored the new dehaians like it didn't even know what they were. The solution wasn't perfect, though. Life was still dangerous. The Beast continued to rage on the land and sea for years after that, hunting what it couldn't find and destroying *so* much in the process. The originals claimed it almost seemed like the Beast *enjoyed* the destruction for its own sake, even if it gained nothing from it, magically-speaking. Lots of people were hurt or killed, just as collateral damage from being in the wrong place at the wrong time. But eventually, it *did* weaken and seem to go away.

"The landwalkers and dehaians, though… they were still worried. They figured that, even if those kids born when dehaians and landwalkers got together *always* died, someday, somebody might come along who wouldn't. And they worried that this person would be like them enough to wake the Beast again."

I swallowed hard.

"But the thing was, they *also* hoped that – if that happened –

it wouldn't be all of it. They theorized that this person... well, they'd been born from the *changed* dehaians and landwalkers, in a world where the Beast's energy possibly still permeated the magical landscape. So while that person might have some of the abilities that the originals did... maybe they'd also be something new. Maybe they'd have different skills altogether. A few of the originals even hoped that, by being something new and yet possessing some of the originals' powers, maybe this person could figure out a way to fix this. Stop the Beast. Destroy it. And maybe even help us find a way back to being able to live on land and in the ocean like the originals did too."

She fell silent, looking embarrassed and yet watching me askance with that creepy, quivering, hopeful look I finally knew the reason behind.

And I didn't know what to do except stare at her.

"They *were* sort of right," she continued, almost apologetically. "You are like they said, at least in waking the Beast. It's still weak, we think, but there've been storms on the coast, earthquakes detected by deep sea scanners... Like I said, the Beast is a force. It'll show up like that before we see anything more. But since the originals were right about that, you know, maybe the other stuff might be true too."

She gave an awkward shrug.

I didn't know how to respond. She had to be crazy. The whole family was crazy, from her grandfather on down. "I... I'm not... nothing's happened that..."

"The water around the boat that day," Noah said quietly

when I trailed off.

Blinking, I pulled my gaze to him, finding him watching me.

"That was this Beast thing, wasn't it?" he continued.

"Sounds like it," Baylie murmured, her voice faint.

I felt a breath leave me. I wanted to run, but there wasn't any point. Anywhere to go or a way that would help at all.

A giant sea thing from God-knew-when was after me.

My stomach rolled. This wasn't happening. There was no *way* this was real.

"What can we do?" Zeke asked.

I looked to him. His face was solemn, and no one but me probably knew him enough to tell how pale, and all I could think about was his family, still under the ocean somewhere.

With the Beast coming.

Niall had wanted to fight it. He and the Sylphaen thought killing me would give them the ability to do so. By taking what I was. By giving it to themselves.

Though that just sounded like it'd make this worse, if what I was fed that thing.

I shivered. This was insane. It couldn't be real. A little over a month ago, I'd finished finals. A few months from now, I'd be starting my senior year of high school.

If I survived. If what I was didn't destroy the world first.

"I'm not sure," Ellie replied. "But not all the landwalker elders are like my grandfather," she continued hastily at Zeke's expression. "I learn from one during the year. Sort of an apprenticeship, I guess you could call it. But Olivia isn't like Grandpa. She believes in the old stories. She'll know what to do."

The words didn't make me relax. I didn't exactly have the best track record with most people who found out what I really was, present company excluded. The majority of them had just ended up wanting to kill or dissect me.

That didn't really leave me feeling like trusting anyone with the information.

"You can't go back to the ocean, though," Ellie continued to me.

I looked to her. "What?"

She blinked at me. "The Beast draws on what you are. If you go back..."

I turned away. Right. I was being stupid.

My gaze found Zeke again. He glanced over, meeting my eyes.

He had to leave, though. Even more than before, Ina and Jirral would need his help now.

"Then I guess we should–" I began.

"Where is this place?" Zeke interrupted, turning to Ellie.

The girl shifted her weight nervously. "Fort Pedrosa, in southern Colorado."

Zeke nodded. "And the best chance we have of stopping this thing is there?"

"I hope," she answered.

He nodded.

I swallowed. I didn't want him to leave. I didn't know what would happen if he stayed.

But he didn't look to me again. His face as somber as ever, Zeke glanced to the others.

"Alright, then," he said. "Who's up for saving the world?"

Chloe, Zeke, and Noah's story continues soon.

Join my new release mailing list at skyemalone.com to keep up with the newest books!

Loved the book?

Awesome! Would you like to leave a review? Visit Amazon, Goodreads, or any other book-related site and tell people about it!

Other titles

The Awakened Fate series

The Children and the Blood trilogy (published under the name Megan Joel Peterson)

About the author

Skye Malone is a fantasy author, which means she spends most of her time not-quite-convinced that the things she imagines couldn't actually exist. Born and raised in central Illinois, she hopes someday to travel the world — though in the meantime she'll take any story that whisks her off to a place where the fantastic lives inside the everyday. She loves strong and passionate characters, complex villains, and satisfying endings that stay with you long after the book is done. An inveterate writer, she can't go a day without getting her hands on a keyboard, and can usually be found typing away while she listens to all the adventures unfolding in her head.

Connect with me

Website: www.skyemalone.com
Twitter: twitter.com/Skye_Malone
Facebook: facebook.com/authorskyemalone
Google Plus: plus.google.com/+SkyeMaloneAuthor

ACKNOWLEDGMENTS

Many thanks continue to be owed to everyone who supports this series.

To everyone who has read these books: Thank you so much for your support and your excitement about this story. I am so grateful to you.

To Vicki Brown: thank you again for beta-reading, for pushing me to get you this story in the nicest of ways, and for how much you've enjoyed this series.

To Tarra Peterson: thank you so much for your thoughts and input, and for all your wonderful enthusiasm.

To my mother and sister, Mary Ann and Keri Offenstein: as always, your support makes all the difference in the world. Thank you so much for all you've given me.

To my husband, Eugene: you make this possible. Thank you for everything.

63969401R00175

Made in the USA
Charleston, SC
18 November 2016